# Code Name: Verdi

a novel

by Elsa Russo

for J. N.

# Chapter 1

To look at her now, you would think she had been a soldier all her life. Right now she's standing guard on the parapet in army fatigues that don't fit well on her lithe 5'5" frame. Her dark hair is pulled back in a tight ponytail and her dark eyes look older than they should. The hard stare, the way she handles weapons, and the speed with which she assesses a situation and handles it accordingly, all speak of years on the battlefield. But she hasn't always been a soldier. She didn't become one until the world went crazy three years ago. Bombs fell. Who knows who dropped them. No one was sure. Soldiers attacked, but no one was quite certain who. In the space of a day, all the governments in the world fell apart. They were taken over by those who preferred anarchy over order. War over peace. When that happened, she could no longer be who she was. She couldn't do the things she had been trained to do all her life. She had to do something else. So she learned how to be a soldier. She learned from those around her. At first she was ridiculed like all the others who suddenly joined this ragtag army. Over time she proved herself repeatedly. And after rescuing five soldiers in a sticky spot with a jeep, a semi-automatic pistol and a bullet in her shoulder, no one questioned her bravery, her aim or her driving skills again. Those who came and tried to pick on her did not last long. The men she saved would make their feelings known and she would make her point sooner or later.

Her name? She doesn't have a name anymore. None of them do. Names are sensitive information now. If someone knew her real name, they could track her. Anyone could be tracked by their real name now. If you searched for her by putting her name into a tracker, it would bring you to her last known location which is a blown out building. But she's not there. She was there three years ago. That was the last time she went by her name. None of the soldiers in her squad go by their names. It's too dangerous. When on missions they go by code names. That's the only time they call each other anything other than the numbers on their bunks. Long ago someone painted a number on each bunk in their room. She has 3. Her best friend sleeps below her in 4.

4 is standing guard with her on the parapet. If you can imagine one 6'3" wall of Scottish man muscle with piercing blue eyes, fire red hair and a laugh that would make even a stone giggle that would be 4. He has been a soldier his whole life. When people started pouring in wanting to volunteer and be soldiers, he had thought little of 3. He thought with her short stature that she would get crushed like a bug. Before anyone else, he began to notice her resourcefulness and her quick thinking. He pushed her harder than the others and she rose to the occasion each time. He didn't defend her when others picked on her and she proved she could defend herself.

4 knew for certain that she was a force to be reckoned with when he looked up through the haze and saw a jeep barreling towards him and the four other soldiers he was on a mission with. She steered the jeep in between them and the artillery fire. They piled in while she took out two of their men and then hustled them back home. It wasn't until they were back at the base that she even acknowledged that she'd been hit. 4 was impressed to say the least. She spent a week in the infirmary before she was allowed near a battlefield again.

The other two in their squad are finishing breakfast in the canteen. 1 and 2 have been friends since time began. But they look like mirror opposites. 1 has nearly white blond hair and blue eyes. His complexion has always been lightly tanned. Sometimes it gets darker in the summer. 2 has jet black hair and green eyes. His skin is always a deep tan. Both stand about 6'1" and both were always athletic. They've known each other since they were children. Not always in the same place but always keeping in touch. They met after everything went crazy again. Both had lost everything. So they decided to stick together and see if they could find a way out of this craziness. They joined 3 and 4 after they had lost two members of their squad. They had proven themselves multiple times in the battlefield and seemed the obvious fit.

The first couple of weeks were tense. 3 and 4 were still raw from the loss. They bridled at having their comrades replaced so quickly and easily. 3 had nightmares sometimes and would wake up in the dark. She'd look at their beds and see sleeping forms there and for half a second believe it was all just a bad dream. They had survived this whole time. But then one would turn or snore or something and it would all come rushing back. Captain could see it was going to take something big to bring them together as a cohesive squad. He didn't have to look far. Didn't even have to arrange it.

All were called out one morning to defend the walls. Their squad wasn't even awake yet. But they heard the call and all filed out fully armed and in their pajamas. 1 called to 2 for cover and 3 saw what he saw. She called down that she would spot and 4 helped 2 cover. She led him in short calls to the tank the enemy was pouring out of and 1 fired a rocket launcher at them. Then she called out for him to get back as she shot the burning soldiers running at him. With the fight done and trouble passed, they walked back into their room and went back to bed. After that, they worked together well. They were always found together. Workouts, training, meals and worship, they always sat together. They learned each other's tone, each other's habits, each other's moods and each other's strategies. Some wondered if they could even hear each other's thoughts. They called them the Blackbirds.

~

It was spring when Captain came to them with a mission that he felt he couldn't trust anyone else with. They were out in the garden sparring. 4 had been a Tae Kwon Do instructor at some point in his life and he enjoyed teaching them this unique form of hand to hand combat. 3 and 4 were sparring against each other and 3 was winning. Even with 4's strength, 3 was faster due to her short stature and was able to wiggle out of his grasp better

9

than the others. 3 was wriggling out of a headlock and slung 4 to the ground when Captain came around the corner.

"Ten hut!" called 1. All four stood at attention immediately.

"At ease," Captain said with a wave of his hand. All relaxed. "I see you're all enjoying the spring air."

"Yes sir," they replied as one.

"Come inside. I have a mission for the four of you. And I think you're the only four who can do it." They glanced at each other with curiosity before following Captain in. Their base was an old school. Their bare feet slapped against the tile floor audibly as they followed him into a classroom. "Have a seat." They pulled a few old desks together near the front of the classroom and sat down. Captain put a folder in front of each one of them.

"I have a very unique mission for the four of you. I believe you are the only four who I can trust to do this mission. I also believe you are the only four who can complete this mission. You have a target. You are to protect that target to the last man until you get him to his destination. This operation is called Operation Nabucco. Your target's code name is Verdi. 3, your code name is Anna. 4, you are Ismaele. 1, you are Zaccaria. 2, you are Abadallo."

"Sir?"

"Yes, Anna."

"No offense, but what's with all the opera references?"

"It was at the target's request. He wanted names he could remember and he said these are ingrained in his memory like nothing else. So, in the interest of keeping things simple, we obliged."

"Where is he and where is he headed?" asked Ismaele.

"He is currently in the middle of the Terzu province being protected by our friends. He is headed for New York City." All four heads snapped up at the mention of the city all four had abandoned long ago.

"New York City?" said Zaccaria.

"I believe you heard me soldier."

"No one has been to New York in a year," said Abadallo. "No one dares try."

"That's why I came to you. I figured if anyone was going to take on a challenge like this, it would be you four." The four looked at each other. Captain remained quiet. He didn't believe in telepathy as a rule. But sometimes in a room with the four of them, he could almost hear them arguing with each other in their eyes and facial expressions. Anna looked exasperated. It seemed that she was losing the argument. Ismaele looked uncertain about this task. Zaccaria and Abadallo at least seemed willing to listen further. Anna pointed and they all nodded.

"Why are we transporting him to New York?" she asked.

"He has a way to stop this."

"Stop what?" asked Ismaele.

"Stop everything. Stop the war. Get everyone back on the same page and come together as a people. All of us." All four went silent and looked down. The first to look up at the others was Anna. They looked at her. She had been the one stalwart hold out before now and he knew their decision hung on her. She looked at each of them and then nodded.

"We're in," said Ismaele.

"Good. You leave tonight. Pack what you need. You'll be provided with a Humvee and enough provisions to get you through the Terzu province. You'll need to pick up supplies when and where you can. You'll also have a radio. You know the drill. Only go by code names. We'll be in touch whenever possible with locations of safe houses and drop points. Once you pass the Susquehanna River, communication is going to get harder. We'll do what we can."

"Understood," said Anna quietly.

"I know I'm asking you all to do a very hard thing. I know I'm asking you to go back to the city you abandoned three years ago. You know I wouldn't be doing it unless I thought this would work."

"We know sir," said Ismaele. "We won't let you down." Captain nodded. All four stood as one and hustled back to their quarters to pack.

"God?" Captain whispered in the silent room. "If you are still around, please watch over them. This is one crazy mission I am sending them on. I hope it works."

They packed in silence. The silent conversation they had earlier had not been an entirely friendly one. But it wasn't the first unfriendly conversation the four had ever had. None of them really wanted to go back to New York. All four had fled from blown out buildings, dead bodies, nuclear fallout and unending violence of one form or another. Once packed, Ismaele waited at the door. All four were eventually standing together in a small huddle. They looked at each other nervously.

"We know you don't want to go back Anna," Ismaele said quietly. "None of us do."

"Let's just do this and get it over with," Anna replied with a resigned sigh. "Maybe this guy has some genius plan and it really will work."

"How many plans have we heard now?" asked Abadallo.

"About thirty," replied Zaccaria.

"33," said Anna.

"All of them failures," said Ismaele. "But we have to try. We don't have any other choice."

"Right, that's settled then," said Anna. "Let's go before I change my mind." All four stomped out of their room and into the hallway. Other soldiers saluted them as they walked past. They weren't sure where the Blackbirds were going or what their mission was. They only knew it had to be of the utmost importance if they were being sent. They walked out the front door and loaded up the Humvee. Captain was standing outside watching them load. He hoped he wasn't sending them off on another "rescue the world" mission that was only doomed to failure. The last time had nearly gotten all four of them killed. Ismaele got behind the wheel and they took one last look at the half-burned building that was their home. They saluted Captain and then drove away.

Meanwhile…

In another place, much like the base the Blackbirds were being sent from, another mission was being put in place. A ravishing red head was sitting at a table dressed in a black bustier, black pants and black boots. Her boots were propped up on the table and she stared listlessly at a map that was tacked up on the wall. Next to her was her boss and lover. At least, he wanted to be her lover. He never did know that she held no affection or feeling for him. He was likewise dressed in black boots, black pants, black shirt and black coat. His skin was tan; his eyes and chin-length hair were equally dark brown. He was sitting on the other side of the table sipping on a glass of wine.

"Did you know that this wine was bottled in the south of France in 1872?" he said staring into the glass. "It's the last of its kind. And no more wine will ever appear from the south of France ever again."

"France is still there," she said still staring at the map.

"Ah, but it is closed off now. And it's doubtful that anyone in what is left of this country will see French wine ever again."

"You never know what the future may hold."

"It is my business to shape the future. You know that." She drew a knife from her belt and threw it at the map. He walked over to the map and looked at the spot. "Is that where he is?"

"No, but that's where hope has started. They haven't said his name. But it's his plan that has reached their ears." He pulled out the knife and stared at the hole.

"Well then, it's a start."

# Chapter 2

"It's going to be a three day drive out to the Terzu province," said Abadallo looking at his map. "That's if we drive 24 hours a day. We can take shifts and sleep when we can."

"We're still going to have to stop occasionally you know," said Ismaele. "I don't know about you but I'm not about to drive on these roads and eat at the same time. We can't afford the distraction."

"So, drive all the time except for meal and necessities breaks," said Anna. "Easy fix."

"Two hour long stops should be enough," said Ismaele.

"That brings us up to three and a half days," said Abadallo.

"No! Call the authorities! It's an outrage!" said Zaccaria. Abadallo rolled his eyes and playfully punched his friend in the arm.

"Just trying to keep us on task," said Abadallo.

"It's appreciated," said Anna. She stared out the window at the scenery going by. Not that one could call it scenery. They were driving through what was once Chicago. Although anyone who had lived there three years ago, would not have recognized it. All the buildings beyond the wall had been leveled. Either they were destroyed by the bombs or disassembled and used for firewood and scrap metal. Every structure had been cannibalized to help those behind the walls that still housed people and the few businesses that were around if one could even call them businesses. More like opportunistic vultures that preyed on the needs of everyone around them. But people needed things. And others needed other things. So there was some kind of balance to it in the end.

"Are there any safe houses to stop at for tonight?" asked Ismaele. "I don't really fancy camping out on the road tonight."

Abadallo searched the map and located a safe house on their route that they would reach approximately by night fall.

"Shakespeare's house is on the way," said Abadallo. "We should get there by nightfall."

"Any other place?" asked Anna with an edge to her voice. She didn't like Shakespeare. It wasn't that he was a bad man or untrustworthy. He just grated her nerves in a way no one else could understand.

"He's the only one in the right amount of distance. All the others are too far out."

"Put up with him tonight, Anna, please?" said Ismaele. "Just for tonight."

"I don't like putting up with him even for five minutes," said Anna feeling her teeth grind together already.

"What is it about him that bothers you so?" asked Zaccaria.

"He's annoying. And he's arrogant. Fucking womanizer on top of all of that."

"Not many of you creatures left around dear," said Ismaele.

"I don't see you three crawling all over everything that moves with breasts. So there is proof that men can contain themselves." Zaccaria and Abadallo glanced at each other secretively and Ismaele chuckled.

"I flirt."

"You flirt, yes. But calm harmless and affectionate flirting. Most women love it because it reveals your soft and sweet side. He's more like a wrecking ball."

"Just put up with him tonight. It's just one night."

"It had better be only one night."

"Fine, if it ends up being two nights you can punch me."

"Where?"

"In the face, silly." Anna stuck out her tongue at him and then stared out the window.

"Fine, to Shakespeare's house. Just for tonight."

Shakespeare's house was easy to find. If you went out from Chicago on what was left of interstates 88 and 80 and waited until you came to what was left of a city, you were close. If you kept driving through that ruined city until you happened upon a blue hotel building that looks at least from the outside completely abandoned, you have reached Shakespeare's house. They called him Shakespeare because he was an actor in his old life and continued to put on plays in one of the ballrooms that had a stage. People would come. Soldiers, thieves, holy men, raiders, everyone was welcome in his house. The plays were passionate and well done if poorly costumed and propped. But people understood. Almost no one had proper clothes or furniture anymore. The happy result was that people concentrated more on the acting and how feelings were represented. Shakespeare directed and often acted in all of his productions. As it has been stated, he was an arrogant and self-confident ass. However, he had never been one so much that he cast himself as the lead in every play. If someone else can do it better, he put them there. He would find himself a place because they are always short on actors and sometimes has played two roles in the same play if it could be pulled off effectively and believably. Among other things, he provided a safe place for people to hide away when necessity demanded it.

At around seven that night, they knocked on his door. Shakespeare himself opened it and peered out. Shakespeare stood a long and tall six foot five and had sandy brown hair and hazel eyes. As always, his eyes landed immediately on Anna.

"Ah, the lovely 3!" he said opening the door wide with a smile.

"It's Anna for this trip," she replied with annoyance already written all over her face.

"Even better. I never did like the name 3."

"We need a place to hide out tonight," said Ismaele. "Can you help us out?"

"Of course, entree my friends." He opened the door wide and allowed them all to walk past. "Enrique was just finishing up dinner. I'll let him know there are four more for dinner. You're lucky he always cooks for an army in case one shows up. You can have your usual rooms upstairs." They trooped upstairs to put

17

down the few things they had brought in. Once done, they returned to the downstairs and went into the banquet room.

The long banquet table remained set up at all times. Shakespeare was aware that his house could be used at any given time for any number of soldier and refugees. So he made certain that his house was always ready to take on any number of visitors. Tonight there were ten for dinner. Four of Shakespeare's actors were having a dinner break. They were recognized by all four of our soldiers. They had seen them in several productions. Enrique buzzed about and served them all a stew he had conjured from the meager vegetables and herbs from the garden and some meat from a local farmer. Our soldier friends were happy to be eating anything besides sandwiches at that moment. Shakespeare tittered on to them excitedly about his newest production. He was steadily slogging through a production of "To Kill a Mockingbird". He couldn't hire children for the parts of Jem, Scout and Dill which bothered him. But the three he had hired were in their late teens and still looked rather child-like when put into the right clothes. Those three were there including the woman who played Calpurnia and Lullela. The man who played Tom Robinson couldn't be there that night. Nor could the actor doing Atticus Finch who he swore up and down was fantastic, or the actor doing Bob Ewell and Sherriff Tate. Shakespeare had taken on the roles of the judge and Boo Radley.

"Considering how busy I've been of late I was happy that I have such small roles in this play," he said sipping on his wine.

"Boo Radley? A small role?" said Anna in disdain. "That's hardly small. Boo Radley is one of the most crucial characters in that whole play. Had he not been there, both of Atticus Finch's children would be dead and the story would have had a very different ending."

"I only meant that there isn't much to be done with either character," said Shakespeare with a dismissive wave of the hand.

"Not much to be done? Every part needs the same amount of attention. You should know that better than anyone. The judge is a very conflicted character. He knows that Tom Robinson isn't lying and he knows that he didn't do it. He has to remain neutral even though he wants nothing more than to break Bob Ewell's neck. And Boo Radley is the most complex character of the whole story! He is shy. There is a whole mystery about him. No one knows what he's been doing this whole time. And on top of that I always wondered if Atticus and he were the same age and that possibly they went to school together. How did Atticus know Boo's real name? He saves the lives of two children and in the end is given the greatest gift of all: the gift of anonymity. He's left alone, as it should be. You're dismissing a wealth of choices that can be made simply because the parts are small and don't take up nearly the amount of stage time that Scout and Atticus do."

"Anna-" started Ismaele, but Shakespeare raised his hand to stop him.

"No, no no. It's all right. This is my house and everyone is entitled to their opinion in it. Besides, she does bring up some good points. I should pay more attention to the roles I am playing and I am sorry that I dismissed those characters so readily. I had hoped to be Atticus but Peter just nailed the part body and soul. Couldn't deny the man one of the roles he was born to play."

"Rehearsals are going well then?" asked Zaccaria.

"Extremely so. Haven't had many problems with raiders lately so most everyone can attend rehearsal as one. Haven't been able to do that for nearly a year."

"Sounds like things are going well around here."

"You don't have to muzzle her you know," said Shakespeare. "You can stay no matter what she says." The others looked nervously at Anna who was now intently staring at her stew.

"They get nervous about conflict with allies," said Anna calmly turning to look Shakespeare in the eye. "Especially if it means sleeping in the truck instead of a safe place like this."

"Hardly a conflict. More a difference of opinion about a play. If I kicked out everyone who I had a difference of opinion about a play with, I wouldn't have any actors work for me." Anna gave him a half-smile.

19

"Survival instinct Shakespeare. Kind of takes over when we exit the walls."

"Understood."

That night Anna lay in her private room. It wasn't often that they got private rooms. The quiet was almost deafening. She stared at the ceiling, trying to relax. That was when she heard a quiet knock on the door. She let out a sigh. She knew who it was. She walked to the door and opened it an inch. There was Shakespeare with a bottle of Maker's Mark bourbon and a rose.

"Can I come in Anna?" he said softly. She nodded and opened the door wide for him to step through. She glanced around the hallway out of habit and then quietly shut the door back and locked it.

"Sorry Shakespeare," she said quietly. "Didn't mean to come by here but you were the best place to stop for the night."

"It's not a problem," he said opening the bottle with a pop. "I think we still have everyone fooled."

"If you're still thinking that you're more of an idiot than I thought," she replied sitting on the table in the room. Shakespeare took a long swig straight from the bottle while staring straight at her. His hazel eyes always seemed to see straight through her and she looked away after a few moments. He put the bottle in her hand and turned her face back to him with a gentle hand.

"You don't have to hide from me," he whispered gently. "You know that." She put the bottle to her lips and took two long swallows while he leaned forward and kissed her neck. She set the bottle down and put the cork in the neck before her arms encircled his shoulders. Being a woman in the army, especially this army, was not easy. Being vulnerable was a liability. Shakespeare was the only one who ever saw her vulnerable side anymore. For a year now they made like they hated each other every time they came into contact. Close relationships were a liability now. The wrong people could use that relationship against them. Her comrades in her squad knew. They never brought it up. They knew their reasons for keeping their relationship what it

20

was. But part of the reason that Abadallo had suggested Shakespeare's place was so she could be with him at least one night. They were about to go into a place that could easily get them killed. They each deserved some measure of happiness before then.

Anna closed her eyes as she kissed Shakespeare on the lips. His hands pulled at her body and she had to fight the instinct she now had to fight back. His long arms gently cradled her and waited for her to relax into his arms. It took longer every time. But she was always worth it. He would never dare tell her otherwise. Soon he felt her body start to ease. Her legs came up around his hips and pulled him in closer. He kissed her neck as he opened her shirt and touched her smooth skin for the first time in a month. His fingers grazed the purple scars on her chest and stomach and made her shiver. She battled with his buttons until she simply pulled his shirt open popping one or two off. He chuckled quietly and placed a calming kiss on her lips.

"Easy now love," he whispered to her. "We've got five hours. There's time." There was good reason for her habit to rush with him. Usually they only had thirty minutes. Maybe, a stop here and there and they were left alone at least long enough to relieve some sexual frustration. Shakespeare had made it a point to ask Abadallo when he would be coming for Anna in the morning. Abadallo knew what he was really asking. So he told him and also said,

"Let her sleep an extra hour. We want to roll out by 6 but we'll live it it's more like 7." The both of them now topless, they began to kiss each other in earnest. Five hours or no five hours, it had been a whole month. For once Shakespeare remembered to push away from her for a moment to unlace and pull off her army boots. With those gone he easily pulled off her pants and underwear at the same time. He had no idea where in the world she had found a razor but decided not to comment as he ran his strong hands up her smooth legs. Her dark eyes were burning and hungry. Her legs around his waist again she undid his belt and pants. Reaching in she found his throbbing hot manhood and gave it a gentle squeeze. Shakespeare held her tight and whispered a curse.

"Long time?" she whispered to him hungrily. She knew that she was the only woman he slept with. But it still turned her on like crazy to hear him say it.

"You know it has been. It's been a whole damn month since I've seen you." She squeezed him again as a reward before pushing his pants down. Then he did something she didn't expect and backed away.

"What is it?" she asked thinking he had heard something.

"Nothing serious," he said caressing her cheek. He toed off his shoes, pulled off his socks and stepped out of his pants that now lay on the floor. He put one of her arms around his shoulders and easily lifted her off the table. "Just want to be comfortable for once." Mostly their sex happened on table tops and in closets and once even in the back of jeep. She had to admit that most of that never did happen somewhere very comfortable. But usually she was having enough fun that she didn't think to care or complain. He laid her down on the bed she had been laying on moments before and leaned over her. They kissed and touched and pulled the blankets around them to keep out the cold. He pushed into her and she arched and whimpered at the pain wrapped in pleasure. It always took a minute to get used to it again. To find the right rhythm and the right spots to focus on. But they took their time tonight. They found the spots easily and then lingered over them more than ever. His hands caressed her and cradled her and worshiped her. Her arms and legs wrapped tight around him and her fingernails dug into his back as the sensations got to be too much. She arched and gasped and whimpered and moaned as he took her in earnest. It had been too long and both of them were soon gasping and near-screaming in pleasure as they clung to each other desperately. Neither wanted to move. They laid together for several minutes before Shakespeare rolled onto his side and pulled her to him. They lay together and cuddled for the first time. Usually they were looking for pants and odd socks at this point. For once they had time. And neither wanted to be somewhere else.

22

"Can you tell me where you're headed?" asked Shakespeare lighting a cigarette.

"Terzu province," she said quietly. "Have to pick up someone." She took a drag off the cigarette he offered her.

"Then we have to deliver them to New York." Shakespeare's cigarette stopped midway to his mouth.

"New York? Why the hell does he want to go to New York?"

"I don't know. He has some crazy plan to stop all of his."

"All of what?"

"This. The war. The violence. Man's unyielding inhumanity to man."

"How?"

"I have no idea."

"So you just marched out of the walls with just these orders? You don't even know how he can help?"

"Life of a soldier. Don't always know why you're going. Just know that you have to."

"And if this fails?"

"Thirty three other plans have failed. We'll go home. Wait for the next big and crazy idea." Anna finished off the cigarette and rolled over to stub it out in the ashtray on the nightstand. She felt his arms wrap around her tight and pull her to him. Her back was flush against his chest and she could feel that he was already hard again.

"Round two?" he whispered gently in her ear as his hand came up to massage her breast.

"This is a treat. We rarely ever get this much time."

"I know. We should take advantage of it while we can."

They made love twice more before they were finally exhausted and ready for sleep. At last she snuggled into his chest and closed her eyes.

"What will you do if this works?" she whispered.

"I have no idea," he whispered back. "Probably wait and see what happens here. What will you do?"

"I've been a soldier for so long now. I don't think I could go back to what I was."

"What were you?"

"Concert cellist in the New York Philharmonic."

"I saw them a few times. They were amazing."

"We were. Once upon a time."

"Wait... does that mean you're-" Her hand clamped down over his mouth and he could see her determined stare even in the dark.

"I was the first chair, yes. You know better than to use real names Shakespeare." He kissed her fingers and held her hand gently to his chest.

"I'll keep your name secret to the grave." She gently kissed him on the lips and then settled back down on his chest. As she dozed off, he thought of the last concert he had seen of that orchestra. She had been the soloist. He now knew where he always knew her from. He had been moved by a piece of music for the first time that night. She was the one who had managed to reach his cynical heart. He closed his eyes and imagined her from that night. Blood red dress, red shoes to match, long dark hair in curls and waves on her head. She was about five pounds heavier then and it suited her. She played the cello with a passion he had never seen before. He drifted off to sleep remembering the notes she had played and the expression of rapture on her face that was so close to the expressions he had just seen minutes earlier.

Meanwhile...

The Captain was tied to a chair in his office. The ravishing red head was straddling his lap. Under normal circumstances he probably would have enjoyed the experience. But this red head was holding a knife to his face. Behind him was her boss.

"You sent your four best soldiers out on a mission recently," said the man sipping on a glass of wine. "What was that mission?"

"It's classified," said the Captain through gritted teeth. The man laughed a bone-chilling laugh. The red head gave him an evil smile.

"Do you know why I keep this girl around? She has several unique gifts. One of those gifts is extracting information from people."

"You can torture me all you want, I won't talk."

"Who said anything about torture?" said the red head in a strange sing-song kind of voice that made a shiver go down the Captain's spine. She stared straight into his eyes and he couldn't look away. His brain felt like it was burning and he started to groan. He tried to maintain his resolve but the more he fought the more pain he was in.

"They're heading to a safe house," she said. "It's the first stop on a journey. A long one. One that goes all the way back to... New York?"

"New York? That place is toxic. Why would they go back there?" The Captain tried to hold onto the last fragments of consciousness but the pain was too great.

"Something..." She slapped his face and he came back to consciousness with a violent start. "Someone has a way to stop all of this. Someone thinks they have a way to bring everyone back together again."

"Is it who we think it is?" She slapped his face a few more times and extracted the last bits of information about the mission from his brain.

"Yes."

"How?"

"He doesn't know."

"That man is becoming more and more irritating."

## Chapter 3

The alarm went off at 6 am. Shakespeare slapped it off with his hand. Anna looked at the time and groaned.

"Why did you set the time for 6?" she asked trying to remember when they were supposed to leave.

"Abadallo said you weren't rolling out until 7," he replied sleepily. "I wanted to sleep next to you as much as I could." Anna rolled into his arms again and kissed him gently on the lips.

"Til next time I suppose," she whispered. She got out of bed and dressed quickly. She was unsuccessfully pulling a brush through her hair when she felt Shakespeare's hand gently close around her wrist.

"Let me do this for you," he whispered in her ear. She gave in and sat quietly in the chair while he gently got the tangles out of her hair. Once he was satisfied that the tangles were gone he tied her hair back in a tight pony tail. His fingers lingered over her shoulder in a ghost of a touch. All the memories from the night before still hummed through his very being. He wished for all the world he could keep her there.

"Thanks," she whispered squeezing his fingers in hers for a moment. She wished she could stay just as much as he wished he could keep her. This mission was probably going to fail. Any mission that involved stopping the war or saving mankind was doomed to failure it seemed. Everyone had an ulterior motive. But orders were orders. And maybe it would work and she could come back here and settle down with Shakespeare and never have to think about war again. But until then, she had to go.

She stood up, grabbed her bag and stomped down the stairs. Abadallo, Ismaele and Zaccaria were eating breakfast still. Ismaele uncovered a plate he had been saving for her. He had loaded it up with three biscuits, scrambled eggs, bacon and a satsuma already peeled and separated into its tiny poppable sections. She sat down, took a long sip of her coffee and dug in. The night's activities had made her quite hungry. Shakespeare's footsteps were soon heard coming down the steps with two female actresses behind him. She knew what was about to happen. It was an act. But if everyone was to remain safe, the act had to take place.

"Thank you ladies for a lovely evening," he said kissing their hands before they coyly smiled and left by the front door. One of them glanced back with a sympathetic look at her. He turned into the room with a broad smile and said, "Good morning everyone!"

"Morning Shakespeare," said Ismaele calmly in an effort to speak for the group. Zaccaria and Abadallo were both still half asleep and Anna had a mouthful of biscuit, butter and honey.

"You'll be heading out soon?" he said pouring himself a cup of coffee.

"Yeah, if you don't mind, we wanted to pick up some supplies for the road."

"I was told. Take your pick from the pantry and the store room. I have several gallons of gas to spare and you may not find any more for a while so fill up your tank and take extra."

"Thanks."

"No problem." Anna stared at her plate as she ate everything on it. She wanted to look up at him. She wanted him. Brushing her hair out for her was something they only ever had time for once in a blue moon and even though it was always a goodbye gesture it always left her wanting more of him. But she couldn't. Not right now.

In ten minutes they had all cleaned their plates and Enrique was clearing them up to wash them all in the sink. Anna and Abadallo went into the pantry with a bag to gather up some cans of food and other non-perishables. Ismaele and Zaccaria filled up the Humvee with gas and made sure the gas cans they took were secured.

"You sure do have a nice ass," said Shakespeare leaning into the pantry.

"Bite me Shakespeare," said Abadallo. Shakespeare chuckled as they walked past him. Anna stole one glance in his direction and saw the same hunger and desire coming from him. She turned the corner and went outside. There was no time for such things. Not now. They loaded the Humvee with what they could and then got in for another long drive. Shakespeare and Enrique waved to them from the door. They headed out for the Terzu province.

"Everyone sleep well last night?" asked Ismaele twenty minutes into the drive. No one answered. He turned and his three comrades were asleep. "Damn, did everyone get sex last night except me?" he muttered. He shrugged and returned his gaze to the horizon. Just as well, he thought to himself, they'll be in better spirits for a few days and can drive into the night tonight.

As they pulled out of the town the scenery changed slightly. What was once desolate and barren was starting to look better. Grass was returning. A few weeds grew taller than the grass. Perhaps the start of a tree here and there appeared. Nature was coming back after man's great hit of destruction had happened. It made him smile. He loved no color better. Green was the color of life. The color of renewal. In his mind, it was the color of hope. He always loved spring. Everything bloomed and blossomed and returned.

~

Spring was his favorite time of the year. When he lived on base he always kept a garden. He grew vegetables and fruits and flowers. He always enjoyed surprising his wife with bouquets from his garden. She would proudly place them in glass vases in the middle of the table. The flowers would stay until they wilted and died. He learned what flowers grew in every season of the year so he could keep her in flowers year round. No two bouquets were ever alike. She loved him and she loved the flowers. She was an amazing cook but a lousy gardener. Therefore they made an incredible team. He would grow all manner of plants for her and she would cook incredible tables full of food. Their dinner parties were the talk of the base. He would invite visiting officers over to dinner when they were on base. All of them praised her cooking to the rafters and would often ask if they could come over again the next time they were there.

The last time he saw his wife, she was starting a stew for that evening. He remembered brushing back her strawberry blond hair and kissing her neck. He remembered how he could feel her smile when he did that and how her body would press against his in reaction. He whispered he would see her that night. But he didn't. He didn't get back home for three days. When he did, everyone was gone. Everything was gone. The place where their house had stood was just a level foundation. All the houses in their neighborhood were gone. Nothing remained. He had fallen to his knees on the bare earth in front of his squad and roared. He roared and screamed for what felt like a long time. But he also felt like there weren't tears or screams enough in the world to match his rage. He frightened his men. All but one. A man even bigger than him who had been in the same squad with him for years now was the only one unafraid. He was the only one who understood that men as big as them, when they break, they break just as big. Ismaele felt a huge arm encircle his chest under his arms and pull him to his feet. He didn't fight it. Didn't have the will to. His friend's voice came to him often in times of weakness and it was always his words from this moment.

"Cry for her. Cry for all of them. But keep standing. We have to keep standing and fix this. And we should and we must cry and mourn every loss that we feel and every loss we are about to feel. But we must also keep standing. We must use our grief as fuel to keep going. It may be the only thing we are able to run on for a while."

~

Ismaele drove for three hours before any of his companions woke up. As he suspected, it was Anna who woke first. She started out of a nightmare with a jerk and he quickly grabbed her hand to bring her to reality.

"It's all right darlin'," he said in a calm and steady voice. "I've got you." Anna squeezed his hand back for a minute before letting him return his hand to the steering wheel.

"How long have I been asleep?" she asked sheepishly.

"About three hours," he said calmly. "Don't worry about it. They've been asleep too." Anna looked in the back seat to see both Abadallo and Zaccaria sound asleep. "I figure you three can keep us going through the night if need be."

"I'll do it. Abadallo's night vision is crap. Zaccaria's is much better but he'll need me to stay awake and keep talking to him so he'll stay awake."

"Fair enough."

"Seen anyone?"

"Not for miles. Did see a bunch of plants coming back. Seems that Mother Nature is rolling right along as usual."

"I suppose Mother Nature could easily roll right along without us. All that talk about us having to replant and renew and she's already taking care of it." They both spotted a building up ahead. It was a long blue warehouse of sorts. But it seemed entirely out of place. It was sitting in the middle of a green field. It was diagonal to the road almost like some giant child had thrown his toys and it had simply landed there. Ismaele slowed slightly.

"Is that on the map?" Anna snatched the map from Abadallo's hand. He didn't wake but shifted slightly in sleep. Anna looked at the road they were on and saw no building listed. Stuff got left off from time to time but never anything that big.

"No. There's supposed to be nothing here." Ismaele pushed his foot down on the gas now.

"Then let's not stop for nothing." They sped past the building without incident. Anna looked back through the back window. All the sides were there as far as she could see. No holes, no tears and no writing on the building to indicate who was in there or why that building was there. Houses or buildings that just appeared were usually dragged there by others. Some meant well and some meant ill. Sometimes you just couldn't tell until you were already in trouble. So she made note of it on the map for when they came back by. They would call the base tonight and see if they knew anything. They probably didn't, but it was best to warn those who might be traveling ahead of time.

"Where's the next place to stop?" Ismaele asked.

31

"Tiger's house," she said looking at the map. "Haven't seen her in a while."

"Sounds good. After her?"

"After her we can get to the Terzu province if we don't run into any trouble today or tomorrow. We should probably stay at Monkey's house that night. He's the one watching over this Verdi guy anyway."

"Right. Any plan in place for getting to New York?"

"It looks like Abadallo is already theorizing on one."

"Any good?"

"Very good actually. I think he has us on a fairly straight line and actually avoiding trouble until we get to New York."

"That's... impressive."

"The man does have the map for a reason." Abadallo started to stir in the back and awoke trying to grab at the map he had been staring at.

"Hey!" he said half-drowsily. "You guys have the map?"

"Yeah," said Anna holding it up. "Was looking for the next place to stop. Saw your path to New York."

"And?"

"I approve. No path is the perfect path but yours is pretty damn near perfect." Abadallo looked over and saw Zaccaria still sound asleep.

"Let him sleep Abadallo," said Ismaele eyeing him in his rear view mirror. "You two can do some of the later driving shifts. We don't need everyone awake right now." Abadallo nodded and let Zaccaria sleep.

They had been up late last night making love for hours. It was the first time they had had an opportunity to be alone together for any length of time more than twenty minutes in months. Being in the same squad they were at least able to spend a good amount of time together. But private time was another matter altogether. Ismaele and Anna they had discovered long ago were heavy sleepers or just too polite to interrupt them the few times they couldn't take it anymore and made love in their shared room.

But the walls of the room were thin and it was hard to make certain no one was listening.

Last night they had been given a room to share. Either Shakespeare knew or Anna had told him or something but they didn't care. It was a room to share with thick walls and a queen sized bed that had seen better days but was far better in comparison to the bunk bed they were usually trying to squeeze together on. Last night they couldn't get enough of each other. To lie together naked in bed and not have to worry about people walking in or sirens to be heeded was nearly mind-blowing by itself. Now in the back of the Humvee, Abadallo found it hard not to stare at Zaccaria hungrily. He wished he could reach over and hold his lover right now. Anna and Ismaele wouldn't care. But an enemy might see. Shakespeare possibly knowing was bad enough. For a minute he wondered just how many secrets Shakespeare kept.

"Let's pull over here," said Anna after a few more hours of driving. "I'm hungry and need to pee. There's some nice shade in those trees over there." Ismaele steered off the road and pulled up directly to the stand of trees she had pointed out. Zaccaria was shaken awake and they proceeded to check the area. Convinced it was clear, Anna pulled out a large blanket and laid it on the ground.

"Might as well have a picnic," she said sifting through their store of food. "Canned peaches, Vienna sausages... Ooh, and some crackers!!" She tossed the food onto the blanket while the boys took their restroom breaks. Once they all came back she went around the largest tree to do her business. Then she joined them for lunch.

"When was the last time you went on a picnic?" asked Ismaele. All three sat in thought for a minute. They did this sometimes when they found themselves doing something they used to do in normal life. It was odd to look back and think of what they used to do. But it helped. The shared memories kept them in touch with what they were trying to get back.

"Central Park," said Anna. "A month before it happened. Eric surprised me for my birthday. He got our daughter from day care. They came to the rehearsal during our lunch break and he had a picnic lunch all packed up. Frisbee, crayons and paper for our daughter. It was a gorgeous day and we ate under an oak tree. He was a terrible cook. He had picked up lunch for all three of us from our favorite Italian restaurant. Maestro let me take a two hour lunch that day for my birthday."

"I think it was Christmas Day," said Ismaele. "The last Christmas before it all happened. Jasmine was working a lot. I was out doing training missions. I finally got back the evening of Christmas Eve. Jasmine was already asleep. So the next morning I took one of our little tables outside and set up a romantic Christmas breakfast under the rose trellis in the back yard."

"You lived in New York, wasn't it freezing?" asked Anna.

"I had one of those tents and a space heater thing."

"Ah, I see now."

"Got that all set up. Made her favorite breakfast of omelet, bacon, biscuits with butter and honey. Got it all arranged outside with some Christmas roses in a vase that I had been tending all year long just for this moment. Then I woke her up. Got her in her flannel pajamas and thick flannel robe and carried her outside. Told her that Santa had a special breakfast all planned for her."

"How did she react?" asked Abadallo.

"She loved it. She loved when I did things like that. Always made her whole face light up."

"I am jealous of every woman who has ever had a relationship with you," said Anna after slurping up the last of the juice in the peach can.

"I aim to please," said Ismaele with a smile.

"I think my last picnic was on the beach," said Abadallo thinking hard. "I was four I think. I don't remember much about it except the ocean and our dog and some slightly soggy peanut butter and jelly sandwiches."

"I don't know that I ever went on a picnic," said Zaccaria fishing out the last Vienna sausage from a can. "Mom and Dad weren't really the outdoorsy type. They preferred air conditioning and carpeted floors and hermetically sealed panic rooms. A couple of germophobes they were."

"How did they die?"

"Allergy to mold that had gotten into the ventilation system." The other three stared at him for minute before Ismaele started to chuckle. Anna reached over and hit his arm.

"It's not funny!" she tried to say fiercely.

"It is!" said Ismaele.

"It is not!"

"It is pretty funny," said Zaccaria with a chuckle of his own. "When they started getting sick, they each thought the other had gone out without telling the other and gotten something. So they refused to go to the doctor until the other one did. Found them dead when I came over a day later. They were sitting at opposite ends of the couch still glaring at each other with that indignant glare they had." Now they were all laughing.

"Oh my god... I shouldn't laugh..." said Anna trying desperately to stop her own laughter.

"No no!" said Zaccaria also holding his sides. "You should laugh! It is funny!" Anna finally gave in and fell back on the blanket laughing uncontrollably with the rest of them. For a good three minutes none of them could move. They lay laughing on the ground with tears streaming down their faces and their sides beginning to ache with every chuckle.

"Why the hell are you laughing so much? You know all this!" Zaccaria shouted at Abadallo.

"It's still too funny for words!" said Abadallo giggling still. This set off a new set of giggles in all of them that left them breathless and smiling.

"We should get going," said Anna looking at the sky. "We've got a ways to go before we get to stop again."

"Right," said Ismaele. "Who's up for driving?"

"I'll do it," said Abadallo. "We all know my night vision's crap." The others nodded and packed up. Abadallo got in the front seat while Ismaele and Anna climbed into the back. Soon the two of them were out like a light.

"You still with me?" Abadallo asked after a few minutes.

"Yeah, I'm still with you," said Zaccaria quietly. "They're both out cold."

"Let 'em. You know if Anna doesn't drive us tonight it will be you and she'll be the one to stay up and talk to you while you drive."

"Only because you distract me too much."

"I know. Never can figure out how I do it but I know."

"It's like a moth to a flame kind of situation."

"Not sure if I really like that analogy."

"Ok, moth to a light bulb. That way I won't burn up. I can't help but stare and try to get as close to you as I can even if it might burn me."

"You had me last night."

"I had you three times last night. Still not enough."

"Well, maybe this will work."

"Do you believe that it will?"

"I don't know. I've seen enough plans fail to know that every plan has a huge margin of failure. Still, nice to have hope once in a while."

"But then it feels like the carpet has been yanked out from under you when it all falls to pieces. Last time it nearly killed all of us. And we got within a hair's breadth of losing Anna!"

"I know. I remember."

~

A year ago, Captain had come to them with a mission to help save the world. This man thought he had finally found the answer. He came to Captain with payment of fuel, food and medicine. Medicine was something they desperately needed. So when he asked for the best soldiers to join him on a mission to fix the world, they volunteered. He turned out to be a mad man. A mad man with a plan and his plan as it turned out was human sacrifice. After drugging them all with a sedative in their water canteens, he locked the boys in a bamboo cage and tied Anna to a stone altar. But he didn't want to start until they had all regained consciousness and could witness the genius of his plan. That was his greatest mistake. The boys begged and pleaded as the mad

36

man cut V-shaped incisions into her flesh. In all there were three on her torso and two on her legs. All of them pointed to her feet and the crude symbols on the wall left there by some long gone civilization. Ismaele with all of his bull strength managed to break the bamboo poles of the cage they were locked in. Zaccaria beheaded the mad man with one deadly strike from his knife while Ismaele and Abadallo pulled Anna from the stone altar she had been tied to. She was bleeding so badly Abadallo wasn't sure what to bandage first. She could barely talk. But she looked at them with just as much fire and determination as ever. Her eyes begged him, "Don't let me die!" Abadallo immediately dug through his bag and pulled out every bandage possible. He also got out scissors and a bottle of water.

Zaccaria watched the door with a gun while Ismaele helped Abadallo get her clothes off and clean her up. He needed to see where her wounds were in order to patch them properly. Normally Anna would have detested the idea of lying naked before them. But at this point she was too cold and in too much pain to care. She was vaguely aware that they were helping and trying to bandage her as fast as possible. Ismaele held her hand tight and told her to look at him. She turned her head to stare at him and he whispered reassurances over and over again that everything was going to be alright.

"I'm scared," she finally whispered to him through chattering teeth.

"I know honey, it's okay," he said stroking her cheek. "It's going to be okay."

"I'm so scared."

"I know. It's going to be okay. We've got you. He's bandaging you up right now. You don't have a thing to worry about."

"I'm cold."

"I know honey, I know. We'll get that fixed as soon as possible." She started shivering as Abadallo got the last bandage on.

"Help me get this blanket around her," he said quietly to Ismaele. He put his big arms around her and lifted her to his chest.  He could feel how cold her skin was next to his and he got an idea.  Once Abadallo had the blanket under her and was wrapping her up, Ismaele took off his shirt and held her naked body to his bare skin, making sure the rest of her was covered in the blanket.  One of her arms she managed to drape over his shoulder so she was a few centimeters closer to him.  He lifted her in his arms and carried her out to the truck they had been riding in.  He got into the flatbed of the truck with his back against the cab to keep her from getting cold in the wind.  The two side windows and windshield of the cab were long gone and only the back window remained.  His position was the only place that he believed he could keep her warm.  Zaccaria got behind the wheel and Abadallo sat next to him in the front seat.  He cried for an hour.  Ismaele held her close to him across bumpy roads.

They had to stop at one point during the night because it was just too cold.  They set up their tent and huddled close together all night.  Anna was sandwiched between Ismaele and Zaccaria with Abadallo right behind Zaccariah.  She shivered and shook if either of them rolled away.  They would soon feel it and roll back even in sleep.  They pulled the sleeping bags tight around their huddled selves and prayed to get through the night.

The next morning she insisted they leave her behind.

"Not going to happen," said Ismaele.

"I will slow you down," she said as evenly as she could through the shivers still wracking her body.  "You three have to get back.  Go back now.  Leave me here."

"No."  The others were not about to argue with him.  And they were not about to leave her behind.  Zaccaria held her to himself while the others searched the truck for some food and for some clean clothes for her.

"Give in," said Zaccaria.  "We're not leaving you.  Ismaele broke through bamboo, I beheaded the man and Abadallo is putting together every last trick he knows to keep you alive.  We've brought you too far to give in now."  Abadallo changed her dressings.  They found some sweatpants and a t-shirt for her to wear amongst their things but when in the truck it was still best for her to be wrapped up close with Ismaele.  He shared his body heat with her all the way back to the base the next night. He carried her into the infirmary and finally let her go for the first time in three days.

That night Zaccaria and Abadallo woke up to Ismaele screaming and reaching out for Anna.

"No!!" he screamed in a voice that they both swore later could have woken the dead and did wake their entire hallway. "No!! She's gone!! Where is she?!!" Zaccaria bolted out of bed and grabbed Ismaele by the shoulders and shook him.

"She's okay!" he shouted. "Ismaele we're home!! She's okay!!" Abadallo got out of bed too and tried shouting at him as well. Both of them had to grab him, shake him and yell at the top of their lungs at him until he broke out of the nightmare and realized where he was.

"What...?" he said looking at their worried expressions with confusion. "Where is she?" he asked calmly and quietly now.

"She's in the infirmary, remember?" said Zaccaria. "We got her home. She's going to be okay." He nodded slowly but Zaccaria saw he wasn't convinced. He was still shaking and couldn't sleep so they walked him down to the infirmary to see her. She was lying in a hospital bed under a couple of blankets but still curled together in a fetal position like she was cold.

"How's she doing?" Abadallo asked one of the doctors.

"She's doing better. She has a mild fever and it's giving her chills." Ismaele walked into her room, took off his shirt, pulled back the blankets, pushed her over a little and got into bed next to her. In sleep Anna turned over and Ismaele helped her to climb over one of his legs so she could lie chest to chest with him, her legs curled between his. Ismaele pulled the blankets up over her like he had been doing the past two days. The doctor started to protest but Abadallo stopped him.

"I wouldn't. He's not going to let her go no matter what you say." The doctor then saw her heart rate decrease, her blood pressure decrease and instead of fidgeting and shivering she was still. Ismaele stayed with her in the hospital for the next three days through fever and shivers and stitches and scars. She didn't fully regain consciousness until the third day that she was there.

When she woke up, Ismaele was sitting in a chair eating a fruit cup.

"Finally back to the land of the living I see," he said with a relieved smile. She smiled back. That night he walked her back to their shared room where she would stay for the next week.

~

"You saved her life that night you know," said Zaccaria breaking Abadallo out of his memories. He gave a cynical chuckle.

"I helped. Ismaele is the one who saved her life. We both know that. I was quick with the bandages and antiseptic and liquid stitches yeah, but Ismaele is the one who thought of the body heat. He was the one who held her through all those long hours while we took turns driving. You think one of us could have done that?"

"I don't know. I barely have enough body heat to keep myself alive."

"And he has some to spare. So, yeah, Ismaele saved her that time. I thought we weren't going to do any more of these crazy save the world missions after that."

"I don't remember you immediately objecting to this mission. Anna was the one who did that."

"I know. I somehow thought... maybe.... since it was Captain asking us I thought maybe he had checked this one out good. Maybe... and yet we know nothing about the real plan. Again. We have no idea what this guy wants or what his idea is. Again. I don't know why we keep doing this."

"Is there anything better to do?"

"There's lots of things better to do," said Abadallo with a mischievous smile.

"Other than that. Is there anything better to do? As a soldier?"

"No. I suppose not. Fortify the walls. Send out calls to the others. Coordinate... something."

"Something? Like a square dance?"

"Zac-"

40

"I know, I know. There are things that we could be coordinating but we're all so spread out and there are so many bad places in between. Speaking of which how in the world did you manage to find us a path from the Terzu province to New York without hardly any incident?"

"It's all about knowing where everything is. And we've traveled so very much in the past couple of years that I know where almost everything is."

"Remind me never to leave you behind when we go on another road trip. We'll need you no matter where we go." Zaccaria looked out the window and saw the sun setting. It was orange and red and slipping into purple in places. He remembered a painting his former lover had done long ago. It looked like that sunset. It had always been one of his favorites.

~

Last time he saw it was the day the bombs fell. He ran home from his job at the insurance firm. Their brownstone was in tatters. Bricks and mortar and dust and paint everywhere. Somewhere in that all he found Peter. He was broken and bloody and even Peter knew there was no way to get help in time. He grabbed hold of Zaccaria's jacket and pulled him down close.

"Listen to... me..." he said slowly. "Get out of here... be happy..."

"No, no baby no!" said Zaccaria holding him tight. "I'm going to fix this. I'm going to get you out of here!"

"It's okay," said Peter soothingly. "I promise, it's okay. Get yourself out... of here. Find somewhere... anywhere to be... live and be happy. Please... promise me..."

"Peter... honey?"

"Please promise me. Please."

"Okay, okay I promise." Peter died two seconds after that. Zaccaria didn't leave right away. He stayed for an hour. He couldn't move. He finally started to move when he heard gunfire on the street. He snuck around the back alleys that he had grown up on. He ran and ran and ran until he found a couple of friends. One of them was Abadallo. Abadallo was covered in blood.

41

Abadallo had been at the batting cages when the bombs fell. In those days he was a professional baseball player with the Mets. He loved his life, he loved his wife and he loved his one year old son. When the bombing started, they all ran into the inner workings of the stadium to find cover. Part of the stadium collapsed and it was only by sheer luck that they weren't in that particular part of the stadium. Once it had all stopped, he was running for the stairs. The others tried to stop him. They begged him to wait a little while longer so they could find a radio or call someone and try to find out what happened. But he was having none of that. He had to find his family.

They didn't live far from the stadium. The whole way he kept wishing that they had run into the basement or hid in the huge cast-iron tub in their bathroom. When he reached their block, he almost didn't recognize it. The buildings were half-way leveled. He had to struggle over mounds of brick and mortar and timber trying to reach his house. He stumbled on his wife's body by accident. He tripped and looked down to see her hand reaching out of the brick. He dug like a mad man through the bricks until he found her bloody face. She was long gone. He realized that she must have been going out for a walk because the baby carrier was strapped to her front. Their son almost looked like he was only sleeping. He tried to wake the baby. But he was gone like his mother. Abadallo sat down in the midst of the chaos and didn't move. He didn't move for a few hours. A few other survivors found him and finally convinced him to move from his spot. They led him along until they found Zaccaria running through the streets like a mad man. Abadallo looked up at him and called out his real name. That was the first time that Zaccaria and Abadallo had laid eyes on each other in three years. Both of them were covered in blood and dust and grief. And in that moment of shared grief and pain, the two embraced each other tightly.

Late that night they were hiding in one of the few standing buildings where several other survivors had gathered. Abadallo couldn't sleep. He had slept too long with someone else in the bed.  He walked into the room where Zaccaria was sleeping and gently shut back the door.

"Who's there?" he heard his friend ask.

"It's me," Abadallo replied in a whisper.

"Hey."

"Hey."

"What's wrong?  Trouble?"

"No..."

"Then...?"

"I can't sleep."

"I can't either."  Zaccaria reached out a hand to him and guided him to the bed.  Abadallo sat down on the side of the bed.

"I've slept too long in a bed with someone else."

"I know what you mean."  Abadallo wanted badly to ask. But then Zaccaria lay down and offered a hand to Abadallo.  The two curled together in bed and were asleep within minutes. Zaccaria had always known his best friend was bi.  They had been together once long ago as teenagers.  But first love waned and they both found other people.  But they had remained close friends.  That night Abadallo and Zaccaria cuddled together and slept.  It would be a month before Abadallo got up the courage to kiss Zaccaria.  Longer still before they would make love to each other like they once had.  But after that first night, they were almost always together.  They traveled together, they slept together and they would never leave the other behind.

~

It was getting dark when they stopped again.  It was too cold and dangerous for another picnic, so they turned on the interior lights and ate cold soup out of cans.  They were quiet for the most part.

"Who's driving?" asked Ismaele.

"I am," said Zaccaria.

"I'll stay up with you," said Anna.  "It's only an hour til Tiger's house."  They didn't talk further, at least nothing that was important.  Zaccaria got into the driver's seat and Anna sat next to him.  Ismaele returned to his nap and Abadallo settled in to sleep as well. But then Zaccaria tapped Anna on the knee. She looked up and saw what he saw.

"Umm, guys, buckle in," she said quietly. "Your nap is about to be interrupted." The other two looked out the windshield and saw what they saw. It was a truck of raiders headed in their direction. Zaccaria slammed the car into reverse, put it into a spin and then slammed into gear again.

"How long to Tiger's house again?" said Ismaele from the back.

"The way we were driving it was going to be another two hours," said Anna holding onto the door for dear life. "Currently, we could probably make it in an hour provided they don't catch us and we don't suffer any damage." Ismaele crawled into the back of the Humvee and peered out through the back window.

"LEFT!! LEFT!!" he shouted. Zaccaria swerved in time for Anna to watch a missile nearly graze her door. "Right!! RIGHT!!! MORE RIGHT!!!!!" Zaccaria swerved and there was another missile.

"Damn it! Take care of them!" shouted Anna. Ismaele struggled with the built in gun port in the door but it wouldn't budge.

"Gun port door won't- LEFT!!! NOW!!!!!!" Zaccaria swerved and nearly landed them in a ditch. The house across the street from them disintegrated. "Won't open!" Anna let out an exasperated sigh, unbuckled and stood in her seat. She carefully peered out of the roof hatch to see them setting up a grappling hook in their gun.

"Zac, when I tell you, swerve right," she said watching them set it up. For insane half-starved raiders, they were well organized and very well armed. This made her suspicious. She waited until she saw one of them brace himself to pull the lever then shouted. "RIGHT!! RIGHT NOW!!! RIGHT!!" Abadallo grabbed her hand and kept her from falling onto Zaccaria as he made a mad dash for the right side of the road. The grappling hook grabbed onto nothing but their lingering dust. As they scrambled to reel the hook back in, Anna threw open the roof

hatch.  She took the grenade launcher from Ismaele and took aim.
Ismaele watched through the window and shouted,

"Take 'em out!" Anna aimed well.  She hit her target and
they watched solemnly as fire, shrapnel, blood and bone was
scattered across the road behind them.  They didn't cheer.  They
didn't celebrate.  In these times, people were growing scarce.  Any
loss, friend or foe, was a blow to those left.  Anna dropped down
into the cab again and handed the grenade launcher back to
Ismaele.

"You think there will be anymore?" asked Abadallo.

"Don't know," said Anna.  "Couldn't tell it they had a radio
or not."

"I thought I saw an antenna," said Ismaele.  Anna sat
backwards in her seat and pulled out the map.

"We need to get to the Terzu province quicker than we
planned.  They might be chasing us and I don't want to bring
these raiders to Tiger's house."

"Once we get to the Terzu province we'll be safe though,"
said Zaccaria turning on the headlights.  "Safest place other than
home."

"Good point.  What time is it now?"

"1930."

"Ok, it's an eight hour drive to the Terzu province.  With no
stops, we would be there by 400.  I vote we make a run for it.
Zac, how much longer are you good for?"

"I'm good for at least four hours.  Then I can switch off with
you."

"Right, everyone agreed?"  The other two nodded.  It was
best to be safe and run.  They weren't sure what else they might
run into on the road.  Ismaele got on the radio to base.  His voice
was mostly a quiet murmur in the back while Anna and Abadallo
put their heads together about the remaining miles to the Terzu
province.  That was when they heard Ismaele say in a loud voice,

"Repeat that!  Repeat that!!  Over!!" Then they heard the
crackle of the radio as he turned up the volume.

"I repeat, home is gone.  Home is gone.  Skip the cat's
house.  Get to your package.  Run.  Hope is waiting." Then the

radio went dead. Everyone stopped and stared at each other. They couldn't believe what they had heard. The base was gone. They were ordered to run to their destination. They had to get Verdi. They had to continue their mission. Anna and Abadallo put their heads back to the map. But neither of them spoke. Neither of them had words to speak. Abadallo pointed and Anna nodded. Abadallo showed Zaccaria the road and he nodded. He made the turn and they were headed on the fastest route to the Terzu province that was left. Abadallo turned out the interior light. But no one spoke. No one said a word. In the dark they heard a shudder. Anna was crying.

"Stop," she said quietly.

"What?" said Zaccaria.

"Stop the car," she said. "Just stop the car."

"Anna, it's not safe-" said Ismaele. But she cocked her gun and stuck it in Zaccaria's face.

"Stop the goddamn car!" Zaccaria slowly put his foot on the brake and brought the car to a slow stop. He turned off the headlights so they were invisible. Anna got out of the Humvee and walked away. Ismaele and the others remained seated. They watched her walk away and then slowly sit on the ground. Her face was in her hands and her shoulders shook hard. Ismaele growled with impatience as he looked around and they all got out with guns drawn. They slowly walked towards her watching the sky and the skyline and the landscape for movement or fire or enemies.

"Get up Anna," Ismaele said to her gruffly once he was standing next to her. She didn't move. "That's an order soldier."

"I don't care," she said through broken sobs.

"You what?" he said half-astounded that she had said that.

"I said, I don't care," she said through gritted teeth and the remaining tears.

"I gave you an order soldier!" She launched from the ground, grabbed him by the lapels and brought his face down so that it was even with hers.

"And I told you I don't care! I was just told that our friends are dead! The only family I have known for the past three years is

46

dead!!  I can't just have it roll off me like it's nothing!!  Right now I am not a soldier!  Right now I am me!  I am upset!!  I need five minutes to sit here, cry, be upset and scream at the world and at God for all those things it has taken from me.  And once I'm done, I will be your little soldier.  I will follow your orders to the letter.  I won't complain.  I won't defy.  I will do whatever the hell you want me to.  But I need five minutes to be an upset human being again!!  So just leave me alone for five minutes!!"  She pushed him away and walked a space away from them again.  Ismaele didn't move.  The others looked to him to know what to do.  He turned to them and said simply,

"Keep an eye out."  He walked to within five feet of her and stopped.  He didn't speak.  He just waited.  She didn't sit down again.  She just stood there crying tears she normally wouldn't have cried.  But she couldn't take it this time.  She looked up at the stars.  Since there were no more street lights and no more headlights and no more high rises, the stars stretched out like an incredible blanket above them.  She gazed at the patterns and remembered a few constellations from when she was a child.  She picked out Orion and Cassiopeia and the Big Dipper and the Scorpion.  She remembered when her father took her out somewhere like this and said,

"Pick a star and make a wish sweetie."  She looked about.  She found a star.  And she wished with all her heart that whatever this plan was, it worked.  She wanted things to change so badly, she thought for a second that if she wished hard enough, maybe they would.  She took a few deep breaths and turned back to Ismaele.  There he stood.  Stalwart and still like Orion in the sky.  He wasn't moving.  He wasn't giving orders.  He was just standing there, watching over her.  Waiting for her to be ready to go on.  She walked to him and said simply,

"I apologize for my disobedience.  I'm ready to keep going now."  Ismaele nodded.

"Get in the truck," he said quietly.  They all piled back in, Zaccaria started up the engine and they drove on in silence.

Meanwhile...

"Do you know where they are picking him up?" asked the dark haired man of the ravishing red head. She was lying on the back seat of their personal car.

"The captain knew," she said with her eyes closed. "The last memories I pulled from him were a jumble. It takes a little while to sift through."

"Well sift faster. We have people waiting for orders. And these people get antsy when they get bored." The red head sighed and continued to concentrate on what she had managed to glean from the man's mind before she left him to die a slow death.

"They're next stop is near Des Moines. I'd suggest we try that playhouse there. The man who owns that place is a veritable treasure trove of information."

"And the rest of our men? What shall we tell them while we go traipsing off?"

"Tell them to head for the Terzu Province. I don't know for certain that he's out there, but it's the most logical place."

"Why is it the most logical?"

"They want to protect him. And the Terzu Province has not been beaten in the course of its entire three year long existence.

# Chapter 4

They drove for five hours before Zaccaria started falling asleep at the wheel. They paused just long enough for Zaccaria and Anna to switch places. Then they were off again. Zaccaria was asleep within minutes. She started to hum softly to herself. She hummed "L'amour est un oiseau rebelle" which was her favorite aria.

For a moment she drifted back into a memory of playing in the orchestra pit for a production of "Carmen". One of her best friends from college was singing the part of Carmen. Her voice filled the theatre and everyone within the sound of her voice was entranced. She was so good that even the conductor would get a little too wrapped up in her performance. The orchestra hits would usually bring him back to earth and he would smile apologetically. Most couldn't figure out what made him so distracted in the middle of an opera. But she and a few others who had known her in college knew the problem. The woman was practically magical. In another time she might have been accused of witchcraft just by walking across the town square. In real life she was devastating to those who came within her orbit. On stage she was an unstoppable flood and none could resist her. She had power and magic in her voice and body. It was incredible to watch her work an audience.

The song was still playing in her head three hours later when Anna scanned the horizon. The sun was starting to come up. In the pre-dawn light she could just make out what she had expected to see. Gunmen. Some were camped out in the ditches on either side and some up on the buildings. They had finally reached the entrance to the Terzu province. She slowly stopped the car so as not to jostle any of the sleeping people inside. She put it in park and killed the engine. She got out of the Humvee and gently shut the door back. Slowly walking forwards she kept her hands up. She heard some murmured words in Nukunu to her right. One of the gunmen slowly climbed out of the ditch leaving his gun behind. The others straightened up now, guns still pointed and staring straight at her. He looked her up and down. Then he let out a boisterous laugh. The others started to laugh. Anna managed a nervous chuckle or two. She was bracing herself for what was coming. Her hand halted a fist to the face. She pivoted and punched him in the ribs under his extended arm. He drew back and was met with an elbow to the nose. He stumbled backwards slightly and she remained in a fighting stance. She heard others creeping up from the ditch but he waved them back.

"Anna?!" shouted Zaccaria from the Humvee.

"Stay back a minute!" she called back. "I'll be just fine." The dark man smiled a large smile and she ducked his next punch. She took the opportunity to land a few blows in his gut and then an uppercut to the jaw. She heard the others getting out of the Humvee but didn't take her eyes off her opponent. He kicked her once in the ribs that threw off her balance and left her open to the punch to the nose that happened next. She wiped the blood from her face and the two grappled close for a few seconds before she brought him to the ground and had a choke hold round his throat. He struggled and the others seemed to hesitate. But then the man tapped her arm and she let him go. For a few minutes they remained on the ground catching their breath and assessing their shared wounds. Finally they looked at each other and laughed together in calm and relief.

"It's good to see you my friend!" he said in his deep voice offering his arms out to her. "We were worried you would not make it here."

"It is good to see you too Monkey," she said with a smile and embraced him warmly.

"Forgive the formalities, we had to be certain you know," he said offering her a clean white handkerchief to her for her nose. She took it gratefully and used it to staunch the bleeding.

"Not a problem. I had to be certain too." She turned back to the Humvee and the laughing men. "Right, let's go! Zac's driving." Zaccaria walked over to the driver's door without a word and they all climbed in. Monkey got on his horse and led them to town.

"He does have a wicked punch," she said testing her nose for a second to see if it was broken. She was relieved to find it was not, just very bruised and would probably be tender a few days.

"Serves you right for giving him an opening like that," said Ismaele.

"Didn't think he would kick me as well."

"It was your mistake for thinking he would stick to boxing. Good thing you grappled with him. That's his weakest skill."

"He never remembers. I always get him like that." They were getting close to the town.

The Terzu province was much more populated than any other place they had been. Mostly they were refugees from Australia. The number of people and houses was almost startling to them. They were used to living in just one building with one set of people all the time, day in day out. Here people came and went. Some stayed forever and some, like them, were only there a day. They pulled up to Monkey's house near the center of the city. Anna stepped out of the Humvee and was immediately mobbed by several small children. The hard mask she wore as a soldier slipped and she smiled at them warmly. One little boy climbed up her body and hugged her tightly. She laughed looking back at the men she worked with. They couldn't help cracking smiles and laughing with her. She slowly inched forward to the house with the children all jumping along with her. The others got out of the Humvee and slowly followed her into the house. Anna put down the boy and hugged her friend Teresa as she walked out onto the porch.

"We were so worried about you," Teresa said hugging her tight. "We thought you had gotten killed with all the others."

"We were already heading here," said Anna holding her friend out at arm's length. "And this time it's Anna."

"Ah! I like this one better. Perhaps you can keep it?"

"We'll just have to see dear heart. All depends on whether this guy has an actual answer."

"Come inside and rest your bones." They all walked into the house and shut the door behind them.

"Well Teresa, what do you think of this new savior of mankind?" said Ismaele.

"He has an answer."

"Do you think it will work?" said Anna.

"It's crazier than most. But it has potential."

"Can you give me a few more details?"

"No love. He swears everyone to secrecy after he's told them. If you want to find out what his plan is, you'll have to ask him yourself."

"Where is this target of ours anyway?" said Ismaele.

"Down the hall, last door on the left."

"Maybe you should go make the introductions," said Ismaele looking at Anna.

"Why do I always have to make the introductions?"

"You have a kinder face. Plus…"

"What?"

"You're a woman. People are less suspicious and more welcoming of women."

"One of these days we've got to run into someone who doesn't trust women."

"Give me your gun." Anna handed him her rifle. "And your back up." She turned back and handed him her pistol from her ankle. "And the other." She turned back with an exasperated sigh.

"Should I go in there naked? Would that make everyone feel better?"

"No. Just unarmed." She pulled her gun from the small of her back, her knife from her belt and her Taser from her inside jacket pocket. She walked down the dark hallway past a few doors that were silent. Outside the last door she heard something. Something she hadn't heard in a long time. She was straining her ears and she wasn't certain, but she could almost swear that it was the sound of an orchestra playing the last bars of

54

the last movement of Tchaikovsky's sixth symphony.  Just the sound nearly brought her to her knees in tears.  A memory so painful that she never thought about it for fear of breaking apart.  She shook off her memories and then knocked on the door.  The sound stopped and the door opened a crack.  She saw a dark green eye peer out through the crack.  She tilted her head to match the angle and waved.

"Verdi?" she asked calmly.  The head nodded.  "Can I come in?"  The door opened wider.  Anna walked in and looked around at the room.  One bed, one table, one chair and one iPod with a speaker sitting on the table.  She was shocked to say the least.  Hardly any uncorrupted iPods could be found after the bombs fell.  And those found were as precious as gold in trade.  The door shut and she turned to him calmly.

"You are?" said the little man.

"Anna," she replied.  She looked him up and down.  He wasn't really remarkable looking.  He stood about five feet and five inches tall.  He had sandy brown hair speckled with white and green eyes that looked older than hers.  He looked to be about in his mid-thirties if she had to guess.  Maybe a year older than her.  Not quite your savior of the world type.  But then no one had looked like Superman or Jesus so she guessed she couldn't judge just on his looks.  He wasn't pale.  He was lightly tan and kept his hands folded at his waist.

"I had been told that everyone at the base was dead," he said with fear in his voice.

"They are.  We were sent out on this mission two days ago.  Our luck I suppose."

"The others?"

"Ismaele, Abadallo and Zaccaria are outside.  We've been driving all night to avoid raiders.  We'll sleep here tonight and start for New York in the morning."

"I see.  Do you believe it is wise to delay?"  She frowned at him.

"Why do you ask?"

"If the raiders are coming, shouldn't we be far from here?"

"The Terzu province has stood for three years. It has been attacked and nearly overrun but it has never been overtaken. If we were out on the road I am almost certain that the raiders would bypass Terzu and come after us instead and most assuredly kill us. We're safer here. If the raiders have followed us, Monkey's men can take them on."

"I just thought that-"

"How much experience do you have on the road?" She was starting to get annoyed. This little pipsqueak, she was certain, knew nothing.

"Define experience."

"How much time have you spent in a truck out on the road with a few other guys and guns?"

"Much."

"Were you armed?" He looked down at his shoes now.

"No. I've been shuttled around from place to place for a while now."

"I see. Always under armed guard?"

"Yes."

"And did you give your other armed escorts this much trouble."

"I did. It seems I have a knack for being trouble."

"I can tell. We've already seen trouble on this mission. Tonight we would like to avoid it. So if you don't mind, we will stay here tonight and get on the road in the morning. Understand?"

"Yes, perfectly."

"Good. Now, come out with me." She opened the door and she saw him recoil from the sound of it like he had been stung. "What's the matter?" Now she was very annoyed. This man didn't have the courage to step outside his room and he was going to save the world?

"I-I-I don't like going outside."

"It's not outside; we're stepping into the hallway and the living room."

"I-I don't like leaving my room."

"You're going to have to leave your room tomorrow morning if you want to get to New York. Might as well get some practice being outside of it." She stood waiting and watching him twitch and falter. "Would you rather stay here and let the world rot?!"

"No!" he shouted. It was the first word he had said to her above the volume of a whisper.

"Then get out here and meet your other protectors so you know what they look like and they know what you look like!"

"We can come-" started Ismaele.

"Stop!" she shouted down the hall. "He has to get out of this room sooner or later and he should start now so we don't have to drag him kicking and screaming out of it tomorrow!" She turned back with eyes hard as stones and it nearly frightened him into abandoning the mission all together. "Now, get out here and meet the others in your armed escort!" He shuffled forward slowly. His fears of the outside world growing with every step.

She grew more and more annoyed with every step. But she held still next to the door. Soon he was standing in the doorway. He peered around the door jamb and up the hallway. Ismaele, Zaccaria and Abadallo had the same reaction to Verdi that Anna had: he was too small to be the savior of the world. He started to shuffle back after seeing them but Anna was standing behind him and kept him from walking back into the room.

"No, you don't," she said blocking the whole doorway with her arms. "I can't even recognize them from here with the sun behind them like that. Go out into the hallway." His heart was thumping fast and she could feel it through his back that was pressed against her ribs. He looked at the ground and tried to concentrate on the cracks in the stone as he stepped forward.

One tiny step and Anna shut the door with an audible "thud". He twitched and looked back with trepidation. Anna kept her mask of severity. He turned towards the front room and began to shuffle forward. Anna was right behind him the entire way. He only knew because he could hear her footsteps shuffle along with his. She wasn't pushing him physically. But he was certain that if he turned back she would turn him around again and keep him going in the

57

same direction.  The people here were nice.  They took care of him.  They coddled him.  They treated him with an incredible amount of patience and kindness.  But no one had challenged him until now.  If he was honest, the change was almost refreshing.  He shuffled into the living room and looked up at the other members of his armed guard.  They were a lot like the others that he had had.  They were soldiers.  They were trained to fight.  They were loyal to each other.  Two were in love with each other.  The other and Anna he was certain were close but more like a brother and sister are close.  They never tried to cross the line into romantic endeavors.  He wondered why.

"Hello," he said quietly.  "I am Verdi."

"Ismaele."

"Zaccaria."

"Abadallo."  He nodded respectfully to each of them as they said their name.  Verdi tried to memorize one thing about the appearance of each person as they said their name.  Isamaele's fire red hair.  Zaccaria's scar that divided one of his eyebrows.  Abadallo's earlobe that was half gone due to a long ago injury.  He turned back and knew that he would know Anna by her eyes and her eyes alone.  She was determined.  Annoyed but determined.  And her eyes were the force that pushed everyone around her forward.  She looked at him and said,

"You've seen them now?  Could you find them in a crowd?"

"Yes, I could."

"Fine, you can go back to your room now."  She stood to the side and he walked, quickly, but still walked back to his room and shut the door softly.

"That was cruel Anna," said Teresa.

"I don't have time for patience," she replied.  "It would have been a bigger problem tomorrow when we would be rushing around and trying to get things done as fast as possible.  We probably would have ended up carrying him from the room kicking and screaming."

"It was still cruel."

"Call it whatever you want Teresa."  She grabbed an apple from the table and stepped out into the morning light.  She was still hyped up on adrenaline and knew she wouldn't sleep for a while.  She decided to take a walk and see what card game Monkey was playing with his friends.  The boys stayed where they were.

"She's right you know," said Ismaele looking at Teresa.

"He has the fate of all mankind in his hands!" she said looking at him pointedly.

"So he says.  So you say.  We've been on too many missions to save the world.  They never turn out the way you want them to."

"This one will!"

"How can you be so certain, Teresa?"

"I'm certain because I believe in his plan."

"What is his plan?"

"Ask him yourself.  He won't let anyone explain it but him." Ismaele looked down the hallway at the door.  He slowly walked down and raised his hand to knock.  But then he heard music.  Music that he hadn't heard in a long time.  He stopped.  He let his arm fall to his side.  The music playing was soft and sweet.  He hadn't heard something that wonderful in a long time.  For a full three minutes he couldn't move.  All he could do was stand there.  He knew it was a sanity exercise for Verdi.  Trying to calm himself after being outside.  He walked away and sat down in the living room.

"Some other time," said Ismaele cutting into an apple with his knife.

"You're not as cruel as Anna then," said Teresa.

"She wasn't being cruel you know, she was being kind," said Zaccaria.

"Kind?" said Teresa in a shocked voice.  "You call what she did kind?"

"If he had been acting like that tomorrow morning, we would have been far crueler to him than she was.  We would have yelled, threatened and screamed and carried him away at gunpoint if necessary.  He would have found it extremely traumatizing and would have hated us.  This way, she knows what to do with him and she can get him situated in the Humvee early so we can load up quick."

"She could have spoken kindly," she said in a last attempt to prove that she was right and they were wrong.  But she knew it was weak.  And Zaccaria's face told her so.  He wouldn't have stepped out of that room if the person trying to get him out had been kind and gentle.  Teresa gave in and began to compulsively clean the kitchen which she did whenever she found herself at war with what she thought was right and what she knew was right.
 Ismaele went out to speak with his friend Andy and check the perimeter.

Zaccaria was still curious about their target.  He walked down the hallway to the door where Verdi was.  He heard the same thing that had stopped Ismaele.  He heard music.  Sweet and gentle music.  It made him smile.  He stood there a minute trying to recognize the piece.  But he couldn't come up with the name or the composer or even the time period it would have been written in.  He felt bad since normally he would be able to pick up on those things within minutes.  He gently knocked on the door and the music stopped.

"Who is it?" called a timid voice.

"It's Zaccaria," he said calmly.  "I don't want to make you come out.  I just want to come in and talk."  The door unlatched and drifted open a crack.  Zaccaria opened the door a small amount and saw Verdi sitting on the bed.  He was sitting on the far side with his back to the wall, his legs folded up to his chin and his arms around his legs.  Zaccaria nodded as he walked in and said, "Thank you."  He shut the door back quietly and stood still.

"Have a seat," said Verdi with a smile.  Verdi delighted in the old social graces.  Zaccaria had sensed that when Verdi had nodded to each of them.  He remembered them and wanted to make Verdi more at ease.  Zaccaria sat in the one chair next to the table.

"Thank you.  I came to apologize for Anna."

"Don't.  She doesn't know you're here doing this, does she?"

"No. She's been a soldier for a while now. Sometimes the mission is all she concentrates on."

"She made a valid point. I am coddled. People try to do everything for me because they think my plan will work."

"Do you think your plan will work?"

"I have no idea." He paused for a moment watching Zaccaria's expression. "Does that make you angry?"

"No. It makes me relieved."

"Relieved?"

"Every plan before this one they were certain that it would work. They were certain with every fiber of their being that it would work. And they never have. When their plans didn't work either we were to blame or the materials weren't right or the conditions or something. But they never would admit that they were wrong. Drove me more insane than the plan not working. What is your plan?"

"Will you tell the others if I tell you?"

"More than likely."

"I'll tell you much later then."

"They said you swear everyone to secrecy once you tell them. Do you doubt I could keep a secret from them?"

"You're a soldier. You're part of a four person squad that if I'm guessing right has been together for some time now." Zaccaria paused for a moment before answering. They were close but he never thought their connection was obvious.

"Two years."

"You know everything about each other?"

"Almost everything there is to know."

"You shouldn't have secrets from each other. It would weaken the bond the four of you have."

"Suit yourself."

"You don't deny the bond?"

"Why should I? To deny it is to deny that it exists. And it does. If I deny its existence, it could evaporate. And then what will we do?"

"I imagine you would go on."

"We would go on.  But we would probably get killed.  As it is now, we can read each other's body language and tone of voice at the drop of a hat.  I know when one of them is hurting almost before they do.  I know when they've spotted a threat just by their tone.  We strategize on the fly.  We fight almost like one person."

"You love him."

"Who?"

"Abadallo."

"We don't say such things."

"Why?"

"You never know who is listening.  They could use it against us."

"Does everyone hide their relationships?"

"Everyone."

"Do the others know?"

"They know, but they won't say.  They don't want others to use it against them either."

"How long?"

"Is every sentence you form a question?"  Verdi didn't move.  He didn't nod or shake his head.  He didn't even acknowledge the question.  He was focused.  He wanted information.  "Almost three years now."

"Does he love you?"  Zaccaria winced.  He knew.  He knew Abadallo loved him with all his being.  He had proved it.

"Yes," he whispered in a shaky voice.  "Yes, he does love me."  Verdi unwrapped his arms from his legs and moved forward on the bed.  His legs were down now, his feet touching the floor.

"How do you know?"  Zaccaria couldn't stop the memories now.  The memories from just a few months ago.

~

It was an errand.  Just a stupid errand to go find wood for the boiler.  That was all.  That was all they were supposed to do.  Raiders hadn't attacked in months.  Maybe that was why it had happened.  They had grown too comfortable.  Zaccaria and Abadallo had been sent out to gather firewood together.  They hadn't been alone together in a month and they would later tell themselves that they couldn't help it.  Zaccaria had Abadallo pinned to a tree and was kissing all the breath out of him when he felt it. The sting in his side. He looked down in time so see a dart and hear Abadallo shout. Then the world went dark. When he woke up he was tied to the tree. Abadallo tied next to him.

"Wake up!" Abadallo whispered.

"What?" said Zaccaria clumsily.

"Thank God, we have got to get out of here before-" But then he saw them. The raiders. Three large men with sickening smiles on their faces. They all looked the same. Dark hair, dark eyes and bad intentions.

"Look at these two pretties we have here," said one. "You boys did good." Zaccaria flinched as the first one stroked his cheek. In response he was slapped across the face. "I'll teach you to like my touch boy!" Zaccaria was untied but his hands kept bound. They pulled him up from the ground roughly. He could barely orient himself and they were moving too fast.

"No!! Take me!!" Zaccaria closed his eyes and cursed as he heard his lover's voice say those words. "Take me, I'm better than him!!" Zaccaria prayed that they wouldn't listen. But to his shock, they did. He was thrown back on the ground and he saw Abadallo being dragged away. Just as he passed Zaccaria's prone body he felt something land in his hand. Something long and smooth. But he couldn't comprehend what it was. He couldn't help. He couldn't move. The tranquilizer was still affecting him. He looked up and saw them pulling down Abadallo's pants. He tried to look away but he couldn't. They raped his lover and all he could do was scream at them. He grasped the item in his hand hard and realized in a flash what it was. It was Abadallo's switchblade. That was what he had been trying to tell him. That was why he needed Zaccaria to wake up. He pulled out the blade and cut the ropes holding his wrists together. He still felt groggy but anger and hatred gave him focus. He walked forward and stabbed the man raping Abadallo in the back. He screamed so loud Zaccaria thought the whole forest would wake and come with him to take his revenge. He pulled out the knife, spun the man around and cut off the offending appendage still stained with blood. Then sliced his throat open to

63

let him bleed to death. The others were in shock, still holding Abadallo to the tree. Finally one snarled and moved towards him reaching for a weapon. Zaccaria was faster. He cut the man open from navel to throat and with a finishing touch cut his artery open. Hot blood sprayed his face for the second time in seconds and he didn't care. The last turned to run but he ran him down in seconds. Revenge, he saw, was the great equalizer. None could escape it. He took the man down and cut his face to pieces before finishing him. He got up from where he was crouched over the man's body. He looked down at his hands covered in blood. He looked at the switchblade in his hand. Then he remembered the reason for all this. He closed the switchblade, stuffed it in his pocket and broke into a run. He ran back to where Abadallo was still hugging the tree. He was shaking and crying.

"Hey," he said quietly resting a hand on his lover's shoulder. Abadallo struck out wildly but he caught his lover's arms firmly and forced him to look at him. "Look at me. It's me." Abadallo could barely recognize his lover through the blood on his face. But the voice was right. The eyes were right. And the expression was right. He felt sick. He pulled up his pants and ran behind a nearby tree. Breakfast was soon scattered on the ground and he coughed through the dry heaves. Zaccaria pulled out a handkerchief and wiped most of the blood off of his face. He was certain he was a sight to behold. He didn't know that the blood had gotten into his hair too and turned the white blond a strange reddish pink. He looked to the cart that they had been loading up wood on. They had a good amount. Enough to keep the boiler going for a few days. There was also room for Abadallo.

"Get in the cart. I'll take you home," he said trying to reach Abadallo somewhere in his mind. Abadallo still held to the tree and was unsteady on his feet. He reached out to Zaccaria. Even covered in gore and looking strange as hell he still trusted him. Zaccaria took his hand immediately and pulled Abadallo into his arms. He held him tightly as his lover cried.

"Why the hell did you do that?" he asked furtively. "Why the hell did you go in my place?"

"You're stronger... than me..." Abadallo whispered through the tears. "You could get us out of this. I couldn't."

"I was half-drugged still."

"I couldn't stand the idea of you being hurt." Zaccaria squeezed him tighter and held him for longer than he probably should have.

"I will never let that happen to you again," Zaccaria whispered in his ear. "You understand? Never. That will never happen to you again. I will take care of you and protect you no matter what the cost. I don't care." Abadallo cried.

"I couldn't... I couldn't let it... I love you too much I couldn't let that happen to you."

"I love you too. And I'm never letting that happen to you again. Ever." They stayed until Abadallo could breathe again. Zaccaria put him in the cart next to the wood and made sure he was as comfortable as possible before picking up the bar and pulling them away from there. He had a three mile walk and he knew it wasn't going to be easy. But he had to get Abadallo to safety.

The guards saw him first. A man pulling a wood cart alone covered in blood attracts attention. They called down that something had happened. Anna and Ismaele were playing cards in the courtyard waiting for their companions to get back. They heard the call first. They both dropped their cards and ran to the gate.

"My God," said Anna staring at the sight before them. Zaccaria was covered in sweat and blood by now. His hair was completely slicked down. Blood and sweat combined in a kind of strange pinkish rain that came off of him now. He was nearly exhausted pulling the cart by himself. Anna and Ismaele opened the gate and ran out to help.

"Where is he?" asked Anna as she ran towards him.

"In the cart," Zaccaria managed to whisper. Anna ran around the cart to find Abadallo bleeding and unconscious. Zaccaria fell to his knees panting. Ismaele lifted him off the ground like he was picking up a doll and held him in his arms.

Zaccaria passed out almost immediately. Anna jumped into the back of the cart and was checking Abadallo over.

"Hey!" she shouted slapping his face. "We need to get him to the infirmary!" Three men ran out with a stretcher and she helped them load him into it. Ismaele carried Zaccaria into the infirmary with Abadallo on a stretcher close behind. He laid Zaccaria down on a bed inside. He started to leave but Zaccaria grabbed his shirt.

"Where is he?"

"He's here. He's home. You did good kid. Rest now."

"I have to-" Zaccaria tried to get up pulling on Ismaele but Ismaele laid a gentle but firm hand on his chest.

"You don't have to do anything kid. I admire your fortitude, but it's going to be okay. The doctors have him." Abadallo woke up halfway through the examination to strange men and points. He flailed and started freaking out. He screamed at people to stop touching him. Zaccaria nearly launched off the bed in full alertness.

"I have to help him!" he shouted as he struggled with Ismaele.

"It's alright!"

"You hear him screaming!! You know it's not alright!" Ismaele could hear Abadallo screaming. He knew that sound. He looked up and saw Anna running into the examination room with a determined look on her face.

"Anna's going in. Let's see what she can achieve and I'll help you clean up, alright?" Zaccaria could feel exhaustion and the lingering bit of the tranquilizer still pulling at his consciousness. They could both hear Anna shouting orders at the doctors. Abadallo stopped screaming. The only sound heard from him now was a muffled sob. He nodded to Ismaele.

"Alright, see what she can do. I want to help." Anna understood what was going on when she barged into the room. She effectively ordered everyone away from him with a few choice words. At the sight of her he calmed slightly. She took his hand in hers and gently touched his face.

"It's okay honey, you're going to be okay," she said soothingly. "You're back here with us now. Everything's going to be fine."

"Where is he?"

"He's in the next room. He dragged you and the wood alone for three miles. He's exhausted."

"Are they taking care of him?"

"They are. Don't worry, they are." The doctors were growing impatient. They stared at her pointedly. "Honey, these good doctors need to help you. They're going to do things you aren't going to like right now. And I understand, ok? I understand. But they have to do this if you're going to get better. Ok?" Ismaele appeared at the door and Anna raised an eyebrow in question.

"If you can get them to hold off ten more minutes, I can get Zaccaria in the shower. He wants to help." Anna nodded. She knew better than to keep him away. Ismaele nodded back and went to clean up Zaccaria.

"We need to do our work," said one of the doctors with a snarl.

"You've already stopped the bleeding for the most part, you can wait five minutes," Anna snarled back.

"We have to know how extensive the damage is."

"Do you want to do this with him willing or would you rather traumatize him further?" She felt the death grip Abadallo now had on her wrist. She ran a gentle hand through his hair to try and calm him. "Wait five minutes and let me and Zaccaria be in the room."

"That's preposterous!"

"It will keep him calm," said another wiser doctor. "I would prefer to keep the damage to a minimum. It's in the best interest of the patient that they be in here." The other doctor turned away in exasperation. Anna nodded in thanks to the second doctor and sat down next to the bed so she was quite near to his face.

"It's going to be okay," she whispered. "Zaccaria's getting cleaned up and will be in here very very soon."

"Don't leave me."

"We're not going to leave you. Don't worry about that for a second. We are not going to leave you."

Ismaele was helping Zaccaria out of bed right then.

"We have to get you washed up if you're going to help with this." Zaccaria nearly fell to his knees when his feet touched the floor. Ismaele caught him and held him up. He walked him to the tiny shower in the corner of the room and turned on the water. He sat Zaccaria down on a chair nearby and helped him take off his bloody clothes while the water warmed. Once naked, he stepped under the spray and held still. Ismaele found a washcloth and some soap that he handed him. He scrubbed and scrubbed and nearly scrubbed his skin raw if Ismaele hadn't whispered to him,

"Stop, you got the blood out. Don't start drawing blood from yourself." He still shook. He couldn't get Abadallo's screaming out of his head. Ismaele could see he was in a bad frame of mind just by the look on his face. He reached in and turned off the water. Zaccaria didn't move. Ismaele held up a towel and wrapped it around Zaccaria's shoulders. That was when Zaccaria blinked and looked up.

"I couldn't stop it," he whispered. "I was tied up, on the ground, half-unconscious. I didn't know Abadallo had given me his switchblade until... My hand closed around it in anger. Even then... I had to cut my bonds and... and then I..."

"You did what you had to do."

"No... no I did far worse."

"I know." Zaccaria looked up at him in shock. "I recognize the look. You reached into a dark place in yourself did some horrible things to some very very bad people who really deserved it. I've done that. I understand why. Get dried off. He's waiting."

Zaccaria dried off quickly and put on a pair of scrubs. Ismaele took him down the hall to where Abadallo was waiting. Anna moved away from her position next to his head and let Zaccaria take her seat. Abadallo immediately grasped his hand tight.

"It's okay," said Zaccaria. "It's going to be okay."

"I don't want this..."

"I know. I know and I'm so sorry. I'm so so sorry." Tears fell unbidden down Zaccaria's face as he grasped his lover's hand tight. "I'm not going to leave you. Neither is she. We'll be right here with you." The wise doctor sent everyone out of the room except Anna and Zaccaria.

"Could you assist me?" he asked gently. "I think it would be more calming to have someone he knows helping with this."

"Let me ask him," she said quietly. She walked back around and stroked his hair. "The doctor sent everyone else out. I can assist him or someone else can. It's up to you."

"Please..." he muttered pointing at her. She nodded and kissed him on the forehead.

"Alright, I'm your nurse then," she said to the doctor.

"Right, wash your hands and then stand here and do what I tell you." She complied and tried her best to help him with the necessary procedures while making sure Abadallo was alright. With his lover next to him, he was far more compliant and easy to handle. They were soon done and he was given some pain killers to help him sleep. The two were finally left alone in the room. Abadallo pulled at his hand.

"What do you want?" asked Zaccaria trying to force himself back into wakefulness.

"Get up here and hold me," said Abadallo quietly. Zaccaria did as he was told. He spooned up behind Abadallo and held him from behind. Abadallo laced his fingers through Zaccaria's and was immediately asleep.

~

"I know," said Zaccaria putting a lock down on the memories. "I know with every fiber of my being. And I love him just as much." Verdi was quiet for a minute as he stared at Zaccaria. After a few more seconds, Verdi got up and hugged Zaccaria. Zaccaria was startled at first. But then he hugged the small man back. Verdi pulled away. They both looked at each other awkwardly.

"I should go check on the others, make sure everything is okay," said Zaccaria after a minute.

"Thank you," said Verdi. "Thank you for doing this."

"Orders. We go where we are ordered."

"But you were given an option." Zaccaria blinked for a second.

"We were. We chose to come. No one else is as good as the Blackbirds."

Zaccaria walked out of the room and softly shut the door back. He walked down the hallway and saw Abadallo still sitting in the chair he had left him in. He could see the scar Abadallo still carried from that bad day peeking out of his collar. He looked around and saw that they were alone. He reached out for a second and touched that scar gently. Abadallo turned and looked up at him with a gentle questioning in his eyes. Zaccaria didn't move his hand. He just looked down at him with a look that he was sure told everything he couldn't say in the open. Abadallo took Zaccaria's hand from his neck and held it over his heart. Zaccaria knew Abadallo was answering him the only way he could here. He took a risk and kissed Abadallo gently on the lips. It was a promise. One day they would be together all the time and they would be open about their relationship. They would have all the things they wished they could have together. Abadallo kissed him back. He knew that Zaccaria wanted to keep his word. If he could, he would.

Outside, Anna was sitting with Monkey and his two friends Horace and Ovid. They were playing a lively game of five card draw and laughing.

"How did a girl like you decide to become a soldier?" asked Ovid. He was one of the few white Australians left. Although his skin was brown and leathery from working outdoors all his life. His eyes were kind and his demeanor calm and respectful. But he had proven to be a formidable soldier.

"No other jobs open," she said sipping on a cup of tea. "Besides, couldn't do what I had been doing."

"What had you been doing?" asked Horace. He was Ovid's brother. His twin brother to be exact. But the two were incredibly different. Horace was loud and boisterous and often getting into fights. When the two fought together, no enemy would last long. Anna surveyed her cards, sighed, and folded.

"I was a musician."

"Really? Rock band?" asked Monkey.

"No, symphony. I was a classical musician."

"You should play for us some time."

"Can't. Don't have an instrument. Don't remember how to play."

"You remember how to play. Just don't want to remember now do you?" Anna was quiet as the game finished and a new hand was dealt. Monkey took it as a sign to change the subject.

"What's this mission they have you on?" asked Ovid.

"You know better than to ask me," said Anna. "Less people who know the better. And you already know. You're just waiting to see if I'll tell you whether I think it will work or not. Two cards."

"Do you think it will work?"

"I don't know. I don't even know what his idea is. Apparently, I have to go to him and ask."

"Why don't you?"

"I don't think he wants to see me right now. I made him leave his room so he could meet the others."

"I think that's a good idea. Been telling people that for days now!"

"Those close to him in the house seem to want to coddle him like he is a small child. I get it. He's very weak and unassuming. Most probably want to treat him like some tiny golden child. He's a grown man. He can take it."

"Another thing I've been saying for days."

"So for now, I'm going to steer clear and let him calm down some. I've frightened and pushed him enough for the next couple of hours."

"I think you should keep pushing him."

"If I push him too far too fast he won't trust any of us. Have to take time with it." Horace folded leaving Monkey, Ovid and Anna still in the game.

"You're just as namby pamby as the rest of them." Anna raised an eyebrow in his direction.

"He's agoraphobic. He has a very strong irrational fear of being outside. These days I can't really blame him. There have been days that I would rather stay inside than even try to find out what new evil might be out there on the road today."

"He shouldn't be coddled the way he's been."

"Right, and break our one last hope of getting out of this. On top of that make a whole slew of people angry with you." Monkey folded. He knew better than to get in between the two of them.

"No one said that this one last hope will work."

"No one said any of them will work. And yet every single one has a whole group of blind followers and I have helped, aided, abetted and then destroyed 33 different hopes for our future now. And for one second in every single one of those missions, I thought that it might work. It's always the hope that something will work out that brings us together and keeps us going." Anna laid down a straight flush. "Do you have anything better?" Ovid folded his cards and stood up.

"I have to go on patrol," he said with a mutter. "Nice to see you again." He walked down the street in the direction of the walls.

"He hasn't had a very good month," said Horace. "Best friend of ours got killed by raiders. He's taken it hard."

"Sorry," said Anna with a frown.

"Don't. He was out of line. You know him. He just hates to admit it." Anna looked up and saw Ismaele coming down the road with Andy. They were talking in very serious tones to each other. Anna raised an eyebrow to Ismaele and he waved a hand. He would tell her in a few minutes.

"You ever think of being with that man?" said Monkey.

"Ismaele?" she said with a doubtful look. "No, he's practically my big brother."

"He would make a great husband."

"He did. And he may again, if things work out." Ismaele walked over to Anna and whispered to her,

"We need to leave as soon as possible in the morning." She began to reset her schedule in her head. She knew she had to get Verdi into the Humvee before the boys got there with all their things. The boys were grumpy in the morning. Having to deal with Verdi and the boys together would be too much for even her to deal with.

"What's the problem?" Ismaele gestured that they go inside. She put down her cards and walked into the house with him.

"The raiders have been spotted," said Ismaele.

"They were spotted in the open?"

"Bingo."

"That's... unusual."

"Beyond unusual."

"How many?"

"Fifty." Anna blinked and stared at him.

"What do you mean fifty?"

"I mean fifty! I saw them myself, this isn't an exaggeration!"

"Why are they in such a large group?"

"Not certain. Maybe they heard about our mission."

"It's never caused raiders to be this upset before."

"Maybe they think it has a chance."

"Don't say that to me Ismaele. You know as well as I do that whatever this plan is, it is going to fail."

"The raiders don't think so. The raiders think we have a chance. The raiders think we have a good chance."

"They're scavengers. They're half nuts most of the time. If they were worried about this mission why weren't they worried about the others?"

"I don't know. All I know is that they are gathering in force and we need to leave as soon as we can in the morning! That I know for certain."

"I'm going to have to start really early then if I want to get Verdi loaded up and ready to go."

"Tell him when we'll be getting him too."

"Oh yes, this shall be fun." Anna walked down the hall and knocked on the door.

"Yes?" said the timid voice on the other side.

73

"It's Anna, can I come in?" The door opened and Anna walked in. Verdi was standing close to the wall. "We're going to have to leave very early in the morning."

"How early?"

"We roll out at 500. That means I'm going to be beating down your door at 330. You need to be packed with everything you want to take with you. Take my advice. Pack light."

"I don't own much and I've moved around a lot. I could be packed within twenty minutes."

"Good. Be packed when I get here at 330 tomorrow. I have to get you out that door, down the hallway, fed and then into the Humvee with your things before the boys start loading up. They are not polite and they are not friendly in the morning so do not expect light-hearted conversation and do not attempt to engage them in any. It will not be met well. My suggestion, do whatever you have to do to be in a calm state of mind by tomorrow morning. Listen to music, read a book, meditate, fuck a goat if you want to, I don't care. My objective is to get you into that Humvee tomorrow and onto the next check point."

"Where is the next check point?"

"In what used to be Oklahoma. We have some well-armed friends there who can take care of us. We will be safe there at least for a few hours. You will have to get out of the Humvee at that point. I'll do my best to find a place for you to hide away. It is going to go like that until we get to New York. Do you have any questions?"

"Who do you love?" Shakespeare's eyes popped into her head and she pushed it away.

"Someone. They don't travel with me though. Have to meet when and where we can."

"Never thought of being with one of the soldiers you travel with?"

"Two of them are in love with each other. Ismaele and I have always existed better as siblings than as lovers. Not a great loss. That's the way it goes sometimes."

"Thank you. I'll be ready at 330." Anna turned around and walked out the door. She heard music playing as she walked away.  She recognized the opening chords of the third movement of Beethoven's seventh symphony.  She almost ran down the hall for fear the sound would make her weep.

"Right.  I've got him getting ready to go.  Where are Zaccaria and Abadallo?"

"They went for a walk a while ago," said Teresa.  "I think they needed some time to themselves."

"They deserve it," said Ismaele, "considering how little they get."  He winked at Anna and she knew what he was thinking about.

~

A month after the incident, Zaccaria and Abadallo hadn't been alone for one minute.  They also hadn't tried to steal away and do anything.  Abadallo felt himself tense every time Zaccaria even looked at him.  He wanted his lover.  He wanted him so badly but couldn't bring himself to say it.  One night Abadallo could hardly stand it anymore.   He reached up to the upper bunk and pulled on Zaccaria's wrist.  Zaccaria leaned down and looked at Abadallo in the dim light.

"What's wrong baby?" he whispered.  Abadallo just stared at Zaccaria's hand.  He wanted sex, he wanted his lover to touch him and make him arch and moan.  Zaccaria climbed down from his bunk and sat next to Abadallo on his bed.  "What's wrong?  Do you need anything?"  Zaccaria had been a picture perfect lover since it all happened.  He didn't pressure, he didn't prod.  He just waited patiently.  Abadallo finally just grabbed Zaccaria by the shoulders and kissed him hard.  Zaccaria snaked his arms around his lover and felt Abadallo tense.

"I'm sorry," whispered Abadallo.  "I'm so sorry."

"It's okay," Zaccaria whispered back.  "It's okay.  We don't have to do anything."

"I want it.  I want you.  I just... I can't..."  They heard the bed springs of Anna's bed groan and protest as she rolled over to the side.  Then she jumped down and started getting dressed.

"What are you doing?" asked Zaccaria.  Now and again she had a tendency to sleep walk in times of high stress.  Usually talking to her brought her out.  But she turned to them with purpose and complete consciousness.

"Midnight shift.  Forgot to tell you guys.  Promised Billy I'd do it for him since tonight is his birthday."  She reached into Ismaele's bunk and pulled him onto the floor.

"Hey!" he said sitting up on the floor.  He looked up and saw her in black and boots.  "Midnight detail, right."  He dressed quickly and Anna waited for him.

"We'll see you at breakfast," she said to them as they walked out the door.  Abadallo and Zaccaria looked at each other in shock.

"Did she just-?" said Abadallo pointing his thumb at the door.

"I think she did," said Zaccaria.  They turned to each other, finally alone together.

It started easily enough.  They kissed gently.  Every kiss was meant to calm and ease and excite and entice.  Abadallo let himself be laid down on the bed.  Zaccaria peeled off Abadallo's shirt and gently explored the muscular flesh there.  Abadallo ran his fingers through his lover's hair.  He encouraged with sighs and moans as he felt fingers and lips and one wicked tongue teasing him and worshiping him.  Both of them held their breath when Zaccaria laid his fingers on Abadallo's sleep pants.

"I'd understand if you asked me to stop," said Zaccaria.

"We're not going to get an opportunity like this again.  If we don't do this now, it will never be done and I'll never get over this."  Zaccaria pulled down Abadallo's pants and discovered they had something in common: nervousness and excitement.  Zaccaria gently lowered his mouth onto his lover's cock and relished in the sounds he caused to fall from Abadallo's lips.  He felt fingers in his hair and heard constant sounds of encouragement and passion.  He did everything Abadallo always liked save one.  Until he heard Abadallo above him whispering,

"Do it.  I know what you're thinking of, just do it.  Please... I want you inside me tonight and you know how to make it good.  Just do it!" Zaccaria licked his fingers and gently pushed into his lover.  He listened carefully.  He heard a gasp, then a moan, then

76

he pressed his fingers just right and Abadallo was almost arching off the bed. Zaccaria couldn't help but grin as he caused such a strong reaction in his lover. He continued his ministrations, listening carefully to all the sounds his lover was making. He waited until he was certain he was begging.

"Please... please baby please... please take me..."
Zaccaria pulled his mouth and hands from what he had been doing and kissed his lover on the mouth.

"Are you sure?" he whispered. "Please tell me; please just tell me yes or no."

"Yes, yes yes a thousand times yes. It's you. I know it's you. I trust you." Zaccaria reached for the Vaseline that they kept under the bed and quickly lubed himself up.

"Last chance," he whispered. Abadallo just put his legs up around Zaccaria's waist in response. Zaccaria aimed well and gently pushed into him. He felt Abadallo tense, so he stopped. He pressed his forehead to his lover's and whispered, "It's okay. It's going to be okay."

"Just, just keep talking to me."

"It's okay baby, I'm here. This is me inside you." Zaccaria felt him relax and pushed in a little further. "This is me. I'm right here. I love you baby, I love you so so much." Abadallo ran his fingernails down Zaccaria's back and squeezed him a little closer with his legs. "That's it baby, that's it. God I love you so much, you feel so good. You are so tight around me. God I love you. I love you. I love you." Abadallo let out a sharp cry as the head of his lover's cock hit the sweet spot. "That's it... that's it, God that's it."

"Please... please take me," he whispered.

"I will, I promise I will," Zaccaria eased in and out of his lover until they came to a steady and maddening rhythm. He continued to whisper to him and he was answered with all the words of love written in the English language and some in the French. Once his lover started whispering in French he half lost it and took him in earnest. Abadallo wrapped his arms and legs around him and relished in the feel of his lover inside, taking him and loving him like he hoped they could forever.

Around the time they both came gasping each other's names and holding each other tight, Ismaele turned to Anna and said,

"Wait... we weren't supposed to be on midnight detail tonight." Anna lit a cigarette and exhaled slowly. "Did you-?"

"What?" said Anna looking as innocent as possible.

"You did, didn't you."

"I have no idea what you are talking about."

"You told a lie. Got us out of the room so they could have it to themselves." Anna took a long drag off her cigarette and stared out into the night.

"You know they haven't done it since it happened, right?"

"I... no I didn't know that."

"They haven't had a moment's privacy. And they haven't actively sought one like they tend to do from time to time. This needs to be one of the most private and intimate moments of their relationship. It's kind of hard for that to happen when you keep wondering if your bunk mates are going to wake up."

"You're a softy."

"I prefer romantic."

"Fine, romantic. You're going to have to make it up to me."

"Get her emeralds."

"What?"

"Emeralds. She loves them. Especially in a necklace. Something tasteful, not too showy. Something she could wear every day to remember you but still not raise eyebrows."

"You will have to help me-" She held out a silver chain with a pendant on it that had three emeralds in a leaf pattern.

"Even?"

"Even." Ismaele put the necklace away in his pocket and took a drag off the cigarette she offered.

"She is beautiful."

"She was worried that you and I were together."

"I take it you told her she had nothing to worry about."

"I did. I don't know if she believed me."

"She believed me. I wouldn't worry."

"Why didn't we get together?"

"I prefer you as a brother dear heart. As my lover you are just too much for me." They smiled and continued to watch the walls.

"Quiet night tonight."

"Very."

~

After a long afternoon nap, Anna helped Teresa make dinner that night. She enjoyed it. Chopping vegetables and picking seasonings were all reminders of a life that she had left behind long ago. They were making some spaghetti sauce. Teresa liked to load it up with lots of vegetables and a couple pounds of Italian sausage. Anna put the spaghetti in the pot of boiling water. The boys were sitting at the table having a lively conversation. It made her smile. She and Teresa smiled to each other. She looked at the necklace around Teresa's neck. Teresa wore it every day. The emeralds still shone just as brightly as the day Anna picked it out from a trader.

"We would love to have you over one day with your man," Teresa whispered. Anna smiled and tried to push the idea out of her mind. If she thought about all this working too much, she knew she would be even more upset when it didn't work out.

"Does Verdi have dinner at the table or in his room?" asked Anna.

"Sometimes out here, sometimes in his room, it all depends on how he's feeling."

"I'll go check." Anna wiped the tomato sauce from her hands and walked down the hallway. There was no music coming from the room. She gently knocked on the door and the door immediately opened.

"Dinner is almost ready," she said calmly. "Would you like to come to the table and eat with the rest of us?"

"Yes," he said stepping out timidly. "Would you mind walking behind me?"

"Not at all." Her face was calmer this time, but no less determined. Verdi walked a little quicker down the hallway with Anna behind him. The boys looked up and saw his slow shuffle.

79

They kept talking and tried not to stare. Verdi took the seat next to Ismaele. In comparison, he looked like a dwarf.

"Doing well this evening?" said Zaccaria. Verdi nodded.

"What were you all talking about?"

"Old days," said Abadallo with a grin.

"Old days?"

"Days before the world went nuts," said Ismaele. "Helps us to remember why we're doing all of this."

"Don't stop on my account!"

"We were just talking about going to a Mets game that as it turns out we were all at," said Ismaele. "None of us knew each other then. And we were all in different parts of the ball park."

"Even Anna was there!" said Abadallo.

"I hate baseball," said Anna in explanation. She put on hot mitts and brought the bowl of spaghetti to the table. "But it was my husband's one wish for his birthday. So I conceded." She took a seat at the end of the table and poured herself a glass of wine.

"Right, so the Mets are playing the Dodgers. Bottom of the ninth, bases loaded, the score is tied. If this next hit is a homerun, the Mets have won it. The guy comes up to bat. He's just a rookie. No one expects this to work."

"Pitch is thrown," said Abadallo standing to his feet.

"The kid cracks the ball out of the park!" shouts Zaccaria standing to his feet as well.

"Whole stadium is on its feet!! Even Anna!" continues Ismaele standing.

"Yes, even me," she says with a resigned smile and rising to her feet as well.

"And every single person has this kid's name on their lips and shouting it at the top of their lungs!!" said Ismaele shaking his fists above his head. "All four runners come in and they lift this kid on their shoulders!! Carry him off the field and the next day all the papers run his name and "METS WIN!!!" in the biggest font they print in." They laughed and toasted each other with their beers and wine and then sat down.

"What was the kid's name?" asked Verdi. The others glanced at each other uncomfortably.

"My real name," said Abadallo. "I was the kid that they are all talking about."

"You played for the Mets?"

"For one glorious season before everything went nuts. Last time I saw Shea Stadium, I nearly cried. Whole place was in tatters and on fire." The others began to dig into their dinner silently. Teresa finally sat down at the table and gave them an admonishing look.

"Are we forgetting something?" she said. The others put down their forks looking sheepish.

"Sorry Teresa," said Anna. They all held hands round the table and closed their eyes.

"Lord, thank you for good food, good friends, shelter for the night and a clear path ahead," said Teresa. "Amen."

"Amen," the others chorused. Then they picked up their forks again and began to dig in. Verdi listened to them talk. He loved to listen to people talk. What no one at the table knew was that he was telepathic. As they spoke, he saw the memories that their conversation sparked. He heard the cheer of the crowd in Shea stadium, the sound of meat cooking on a grill and the screams of Abadallo when he was raped. He knew from the minute they had entered the house that they were a solid group of individuals. They were in control of themselves and kept a firm hand on each other. They were soldiers. They knew what to do and when. He was certain they were the right people to take him to New York. He hoped for their sake that his plan would work. He saw Teresa and Ismaele glance at each other across the table. He could feel the love and passion pouring out of Ismaele's heart for her. He hoped they would get a chance to be together that night. Anna thought of a man with green eyes and hoped that he was alright. That night she would sneak out to the radio and try to get in touch. Abadallo and Zaccaria wanted to be together always. All of them, in that moment, were hopeful. He hoped he didn't let them down.

That night, Anna snuck out to the Humvee and got on the radio to Shakespeare's house.

"Blackbird to the Globe Theatre, over?" she said quietly into the radio. There was a crackle and static on the other end. "Blackbird to the Globe Theatre, over?" She waited. She waited another five minutes before picking up the radio again and whispering. "Blackbird to the Globe Theatre, over?" Finally a voice whispered through.

"Globe Theatre to Blackbird, God Anna is that you? Over." She recognized Shakespeare's voice even through the thick of the static.

"Yeah, Shakespeare, it's me. Over."

"We heard about home. We're all really sorry. Over."

"Just have to do what they ordered us to do last. Over."

"Stay safe. Over."

"You too. Over and out." She put down the radio and pushed away tears of relief from her cheeks. She climbed out and went into the house. She went into the house and went upstairs to sleep.

## Meanwhile...

Shakespeare let go of the radio with shaking fingers.

"Where are they?" asked the man with dark hair. He was holding a gun to Shakespeare's temple.

"I really don't know how to say this more clearly," said Shakespeare in an irritated tone. "I don't know where they are. I don't know where they're headed. And I don't know what they're trying to do." The red head appeared from the shadows. Her high heels clicked on the cement. Shakespeare looked her up and down. "Really nice look. I take it you're the good cop who's coming in now to sweeten me up and get the information from me."

"Oh no, no he was the good cop all along," she said stroking his cheek in a way that made his skin crawl. "I'm the worst thing you've ever met." His hands wrapped tight around the arms of his chair. He could feel what she was doing. He tried to build the walls in his mind to keep her away from what he knew. She pursed her lips and said, "Now that's rude. Putting a gold mine of knowledge like that behind cold stone walls. That's going to make this even worse." He looked in front of him and saw his sister. She was lying on the floor in a crumpled heap. She was bruised, broken and bleeding. Her blond hair was caked in blood as her blue eyes looked up at him. Begging him.

"That's not real," he whispered. He had last seen her the day the bombs fell. "That's not real!"

"But in your mind it is," said the red head in a voice that sounded like a purr.

"No!! It's not real!!!" He was crying and screaming and staring at the illusion of his sister as the information he had tried too hard to protect was pulled from him.

"They've gone to the Terzu province to pick him up." The red head and the dark haired man stared at each other meaningfully.

"I'll radio our men who are near there. Maybe they can delay them long enough that we can get there."

"Don't count on it. What should we do with him?"

"Do to him what you did to the other." The red head's mouth slowly curled into an evil grin.

## Chapter 5

Ismaele and Teresa were washing dishes in the kitchen when Anna went to bed that night.

"How have you been darling?" he asked her as he dried the dishes and put them away in the cupboard.

"Doing well. Worried as always. You are always so far away."

"Sorry love. You know that I have to take care of my comrades."

"And you know my family lives here." It was an old argument. No one won. But now that the base that Ismaele and the others had called home was gone, she wanted to bring this up again. "You don't have a home anymore."

"We'll go to the next base."

"Do you know of one already?"

"Probably one out in Montana."

"That's even further out than before."

"I don't have control over that."

"Why don't you?"

"Please Teresa; I've explained this to you."

"You don't have to be a soldier. You could leave. It's a volunteer organization."

"And do what? Farm for the rest of my life while the world goes down?!"

"So the whole army will fail because you are not there?!"

"I didn't say that! I don't know that! No one knows that!! All I know is what I can do and I know that I can help and I know that I can make a difference THIS WAY! I can't just sit here and let others do all this fighting for me!"

"So we're lazy?" Ismaele sighed and sat down in a chair. He hated this fight. It was never fair.

"Stop twisting my words, for the love of God Teresa you know I hate that-"

"You keep going on and on about how you are so important that you have to go fight instead of being with the woman you love. You just have to go out and play soldier and be this angry little kid stomping on-" In a flash he did it. He didn't realize he'd done it until it was too late. He grabbed the knife from the counter, pushed her into the counter and held the knife to her throat and shouted,

"SHUT UP YOU DUMB BITCH!"

"ISMAELE!" shouted a voice from above. He was staring at Teresa's terrified face and he knew he had stepped too far. His eyes slowly turned upwards. Anna was standing on the upper landing looking down at him. "Put down the knife now Ismaele or I swear I will cut you to pieces with it." Ismaele backed away from Teresa and put the knife down on the counter. "Take a walk. Now." He didn't say a word. He didn't look at either of them. He had been millimeters away from killing the woman he loved. And he didn't think that was something he could take back. He walked to the front door, opened it, walked through and then softly shut it behind him.

It was dark outside. There were a few still about. But they were all rushing to get home. He didn't care. He wanted to be alone. He walked down the street slowly. For ten seconds, a brutal ten seconds, he had become his father. The brutal snarling self-hating alcoholic who had made his childhood and teenage years a nightmare. He enlisted in the army when he was 18 to get away from the bastard. His grades weren't bad but they weren't good enough for a full scholarship either. They were broke. And the choice of either working for his father on the farm or training to be a soldier was an easy one. He left. He learned how to handle his temper and rage. It was a part of him. Denying it only made it worse. Accepting it and learning to work with it was the only choice. Now and again he still lost his temper. Usually he was able to maintain until he got to a safe place to release his anger. But the stress of the mission, the importance of it, the fight the day before, the gathering raiders and the mood amongst the

86

group in general had set him more on edge than usual. He had lost it. And he struck out at the person he loved most in the world. He continued to walk down the street. He half expected Teresa to follow but knew that either she wouldn't want to or Anna would stop her. If he wanted to talk to anyone right now, it would be Anna. He was soon standing in front of the only bar in town. He knew better. But he went in anyway. Nothing would be solved. Maybe things would be made worse. But he didn't really care anymore.

Anna slowly came down the stairs in the now dead quiet of the house. Teresa was crouched on the kitchen floor softly crying. Anna looked at her watch and saw that it was nearly midnight. She knew she would be up from now on until they got in the Humvee. Maybe Verdi wouldn't need her as much as she thought and she might be able to get a nap. She walked through the living room/dining room and into the kitchen. There she knelt in front of Teresa and gently put her arms and shawl around her. Teresa held on tight to Anna's shoulders as she shook with tears.

"Why?" Teresa whimpered eventually. "Why did he do that? We've had that argument so many times..." Anna clamped down her desire to admonish Teresa for asking him to do something she knew he could not do and for stomping so wantonly on his heart and said,

"Not a good time. He's under a lot of stress right now with everything that's going on. It's got him on edge more than usual." She gently pushed Teresa away from her so they could look each other in the eye. "Besides, you know him. He takes duty, even in this volunteer army, very seriously. Army is family to him. It was the first family that ever accepted him and loved him for who he was. And it taught him how to be the good man he is today. And even if this does work, I expect he will still be in the army. If you want to keep him, you are going to have to learn to live with that. Or else, let him go." Anna could never be gentle for long to people who were striking those closest to her. She saw Teresa getting mad at her now. But it was a resigned kind of anger. Teresa knew all this. Just had a hard time accepting it as truth.

"Are you going after him?"

"In a while. Have to let him cool off first. If he draws a knife on me, I'll gut him with it." Anna smiled a perverse kind of smile and Teresa couldn't help but laugh. Anna stood and offered a hand. Teresa took it and together they finished the dishes. After a while, Anna sent Teresa to bed, made certain her pistol was loaded, put on her boots over her rubber ducky sleep pants and went out into the night to find Ismaele.

She didn't have to look long. There was only one bar in town. While she didn't think he would fall that far, she heard a great amount of ruckus from inside and figured that was most likely where he had landed. Two people went flying out the doors against their will and now she was certain. She walked in and the place went silent. It was not every day that a woman entered this establishment at one in the morning dressed only in army boots, rubber ducky sleep pants, a black t-shirt and a large purple lace shawl wrapped around her shoulders. Were it not for the boots and the gun at her waistband she might have looked like someone who just wandered over from the slumber party next door to demand they keep it down. Ismaele was sitting at the bar drinking shots. She wasn't sure how drunk he had managed to get in the space of an hour but she was pretty certain he was very drunk.

"Ismaele," she said in a stern voice. He turned and looked at her.

"Ah, the great 3," he said with a wobble. "No wait, it's Meredith... no no, Christine... no... it's something short this time. Very short... ummm...."

"Anna."

"Yes, Anna. So many have said they like this name on you. I like it too. It suits you. Maybe, no matter how bad this mission fails, you should keep this name."

"Who says it's going to fail?" Anna motioned to the men in the room to leave. One by one they slipped out.

"I say it's going to fail. We both know it's going to fail. Why not accept the inevitable?"

"Because it might work."

88

"Right. It might work. Remember the last time?"

"I remember. I carry the scars."

"We thought that might work. Until the guy went completely nuts on us."

"He was already completely nuts. Just good at hiding it." The last three people left. Only Anna, Ismaele and Monkey, who was bartending that night, remained.

"What if that's the same case here?"

"I believe we could take on the five foot five agoraphobic shrimp if need be. Wouldn't really be that hard in the end."

"I did something tonight. Something I have never done before."

"I know. I saw."

"How is she?"

"She's upset. She's mad."

"And she's afraid of me." Anna wasn't going to say that phrase even though it needed to be said. She had decided to wait until he was sober. But sober was a long way off.

"Yes, she is."

"I swore a long time ago that I would never become my father."

"So you decided to come here and drink until you were nothing like him?" She knew she had stung him. She intended to. He threw down the shot glass. The broken glass made a light tinkling crash across the floor as he pulled his knife. She was faster, threw her shawl onto a nearby chair and pulled her pistol. "Don't try it. Don't. If you want to fight, put down the knife and I'll put down my gun and we'll fight. Otherwise, just don't." He considered it. He considered going at her with the knife anyway but knew she would shoot him as sure as she was standing there. So he put down the knife on the bar. She put down the gun on the bar. He stood with a bit of a wobble and approached. She got into her defensive stance and waited. He was drunk. Too drunk for this. She had hoped that he would back off. But he never did know when to back off once he was this drunk. She had seen this before. She hated when he was like this. Ismaele angry and charging and screaming was easier to take than Ismaele drunk.

He threw the first punch. She ducked. The force of the punch threw him face first into the bar. She adjusted her position and waited. He shook himself and wiped the blood from his nose with his hand. He focused his attention on her again. He walked forward and kicked at her chest but came up short. She grabbed his boot with both hands and pushed him off balance. He crashed into the bar stools this time. She adjusted and waited. Ismaele got up again looking more dazed and angry than before. He took in a few deep breaths trying to clear his head and with a roar charged at her. She punched him in the shoulder as she stepped to the side and sent him sprawling into the tables and chairs. This time he was out. She let out a heavy sigh looking down at him on the floor.

"I really hate it when you do this," she said to his unconscious body. She picked up her shawl and wrapped it around her shoulders again. "Can I have a drink Monkey?" she asked sitting at the bar and lighting a cigarette. He poured her a scotch in a glass while she got out a small pad of paper. She wrote down the damages they had caused to the place. She sipped on her scotch and double checked the list. "Would you say that's a fair assessment of what we've done tonight?" she asked turning the pad around for Monkey to see. He looked it down and nodded.

"I'd say that's about right." He put down a nearly full bottle of scotch. "Add on this." She smirked and added the bottle to the list. Next to it she wrote "collateral damage." Monkey got another glass and poured himself a scotch. "Do I get to know why he came in here and got blind drunk?"

"He and Teresa got into an argument. It wasn't a new argument. She stomped on places in his heart that no one is allowed. And he... overreacted."

"Overreacted?"

"Put simply I saw him with a knife to Teresa's throat. I don't think he would have done anything else but I told him to back away and get out of the house anyway. I knew Teresa didn't want him there."

"He's never done that before."

"No, he never has.  Only people I've ever seen him threaten with a knife were enemies.  But it has to do with history and family and a temper.  His father was a mean drunk.  I once saw a collection of scars on his hip.  I asked him what had happened and he said he forgot to take out the garbage.  Because of that, his father made him take the garbage can out to the street and back to the house ten times and each time he got back to the house, he would burn the kid with his cigarette.  He had to go through a few cigarettes.  After that, I didn't ask about any of his other scars.  He's volunteered the story on a few here and there.  And believe me those stories will keep you up at night."

"Is this why he became a soldier?"

"He wanted to learn to control his rage, he told me.  He learned Tae Kwon Do while in the military.  He studied everything he could get his hands on.  Eventually, he made peace with his rage.  Only came out of him when he was on the attack."

"So why tonight?"

"We're highly stressed and people keep trying to convince us that this will work.  Last time, didn't turn out well."

"What happened the last time?"

"I nearly died.  The new savior of the world promised us that he had a plan that was sure to work.  He brought us a year's worth of supplies and bought our assistance like several before him have.  As it turned out, his plan was human sacrifice.  He drugged us and he tried to carry out his plan by tying me to a stone altar and cutting me up.  I don't remember much after he started cutting, just bits and pieces and what I've been told.  I'm told they broke out of the cage they had been trapped in, killed the man and proceeded to bind up my wounds and made their escape with me.  I lost a lot of blood and it was pitch cold.  We only had a pick-up truck with blown out windows except for the back one.  They said Ismaele sat in the bed against the back with me wrapped tight in his arms.  He kept me warm the whole way home for three days.  Once in the infirmary things get fuzzier.  I remember being cold and in pain for three more days.  They say he was there for that too but I don't remember any of it.  Fever they say.  The scars are the only things that remind me that it

91

really happened." She pushed her shawl and shirt off one shoulder and he saw the deep purple scar that cut across from her shoulder down her chest.

"How many scars did you gain?" he asked reverently touching the scar.

"Ten in all. And gaining them hurt like hell. We haven't been out on a save the world mission since. None of the boys want to see me dead. And I've been rather gun shy about going out far from the base."

"I'm surprised you agreed to this mission at all."

"You and me both. But, it's been a while since we've had any kind of hope. The boys wanted to go. They wouldn't unless I did too. So the decision was left up to me. I knew we had to go. What if it did work? What if this was the way to end this all? I figured if I got a bad vibe, I would be able to convince the others to give it up."

"And?"

"So far, I think the guy has an idea. I think it's a viable idea for him and the others to believe so vehemently in it. I don't think he's going to cause me more scars. At least not intentionally. I can live with that."

"How long ago did this mission that gave you those scars happen?"

"A year ago. I've only been out of the walls a few other times besides now. And then not this far. It's not easy to step out anymore." They both heard a groan and turned to look at Ismaele. He rolled over but then went back to sleep. Anna finished her scotch and poured another one. "Might as well." Monkey poured himself one as well and they toasted each other before downing their drinks. She looked at her watch and saw that it was 2 am. "I have to get Verdi up and out of his room soon. Get him fed and get him in the Humvee. Then get this sorry bastard at least into the Humvee, even if I have to load him in the back. Then the boys have to get up. Abadallo is going to have to drive. There's no way I'm doing it now."

"Busy day."

"Yeah, gettin' busier all the time." She downed one last shot and looked at Ismaele again. "You think he's done for a while or should I stay and see if he wakes?"

"I think you got him good with that last hit. He should be out a few hours."

"Probably until we get on the road. We should go ahead and load him in the back of the Humvee."

"I have a wheelbarrow."

"That will work." Monkey went into the backroom and brought out a large wheelbarrow that had seen better days. She helped him heft Ismaele into the wheelbarrow and walked with him with a drunken wobble to the Humvee where it was parked in front of Monkey's house. She carried the bottle of scotch with her, already certain of its hiding place in the vehicle. She opened the back hatch and they rolled Ismaele into the back of the vehicle. She reached into the vehicle and pulled open the side compartment and put in the bottle. She shut it back certain that it would be safe. She looked at her watch again. It was 2:15. They both heard a man running down the road and yelling out for Monkey. Monkey ran around the Humvee and spoke to the man quickly and urgently in Nukunu. She didn't know what they were saying but she was certain that whatever they were saying was not good. Monkey ran back to her and said,

"The raiders are moving. All fifty of them."

"Could this day get any worse?" she shouted to the sky. An explosion shook the ground beneath their feet. They both ducked behind the Humvee but they could see the flame and smoke column from where they were. Their gas pump to the town had been blown. "I really shouldn't have said that." Monkey and Anna looked at each other and nodded. They each had things to do. Anna slammed the Humvee shut and ran into the house which was no easy feat on drunken legs like hers. Teresa was coming out of her room with sleepy eyes and a green shawl around her shoulders as well.

"What's going on?" she asked rubbing her eyes.

"Raiders are coming. Get into the basement and stay there until Monkey comes to get you. I have to get everyone out and loaded."

"Wait Anna!"

"What?!"

"Where's Ismaele?"

"He's dead drunk and passed out in the back of the Humvee." She took the stairs two at a time and tripped on the last one landing with a horrible thud. She was glad for a moment that she was so drunk because it wouldn't hurt until tomorrow. She banged on the door of the room that Abadallo and Zaccaria were sleeping in and shouted,

"Stop whatever the hell you're doing, get your clothes on and get your things into the truck! You have two minutes!!" Zaccaria appeared at the door stuffing his shirt into black pants.

"What's happening?"

"Raiders. They're attacking now. We have to run."

"Are you drunk?"

"Very. No time to explain now. Just get what you need and let's run."

"What about Verdi?"

"If I have to I will drag him out kicking and screaming!" She ran into her room and grabbed her bag that she always kept packed. She went out to the Humvee and with Abadallo and Zaccaria threw everything in around and on top of Ismaele. Zaccaria started to ask what had happened but Anna said,

"Don't ask me about that either." She gave him the keys. "You're driving. Abadallo, check the map and get us a way out of here quickly. I'll get the agoraphobe." She ran back into the house to find Teresa standing there waiting for her.

"Give Ismaele this," she said holding out her emerald necklace to Anna.

"Teresa, he didn't mean it, don't throw him away-"

"Tell him if this works and he can come back to me, he can give it back to me. He can be in this army here. I don't care. He can be a soldier."

"Teresa please don't-"

94

"Please do this Anna. You're the only one he'll listen to. You know that." She didn't have time to argue. She took the necklace and said to her,

"Mark my words, if this causes his death, I will blame you." She put the necklace on her neck and walked to Verdi's door. She heard Teresa start to cry as she ran down the hall. She banged on Verdi's door and when she didn't get an answer she walked in. She saw the problem. Verdi was lying on his bed with headphones in his ears. She walked over to him and ripped the ear buds out of his ears. He launched off the bed with a jolt and stared at her with frightened eyes.

"Are you packed?" she said in a forceful voice.

"Yes, I packed last night, why-"

"Do not ask questions. I don't have time. The raiders are coming right now. They are coming to attack this place. Monkey and his men can keep them busy long enough for us to escape and put a big dent in their forces so they can't give chase. I need to get you and your stuff into the Humvee now." She could see it. She could see the fear already starting to take over his every bodily movement and function. "This is what we're going to do. You're going to put these ear buds back in and turn it up as loud as you dare. Pick your favorite piece. I'm going to blindfold you so you don't see anything. I'll carry your bag. You just hold my hand and move where I push and pull you to. Do you understand?" He nodded mutely. He didn't like the plan. But it was better than staying there and dying. She put the ear buds securely back into his ears. He looked down at his iPod and started up the 1812 Overture. She took a decorative piece of fabric from the chest of drawers and wrapped it around his eyes and ears. She picked up his bag that he had been gesturing to earlier and took him by the hand. Not seeing anything, he actually moved faster like a blindfolded horse through fire. She tossed his bag in the back with the others and turned him around. Zaccaria and Abadallo lifted him into the Humvee and got him secure in a seat.

"What's with the blindfold?" asked Zaccaria.

"You know a better way to get him here this fast?" The others didn't have an answer. They understood now. Anna crawled into the back and opened the window. Zaccaria got in the driver's seat and Abadallo sat with the map and a pen.

"We can get to safe passage through the southwest end of the province," he said. "That would probably be-" Zaccaria and Abadallo both saw the same thing.

"What is it?" Anna asked looking up. Then she saw what they saw. "Get him down!" It was three attack trucks very similar to one they'd fought the day before. Only the men on the trucks had automatic weapons and flame throwers. They were shooting and lighting up the place. Monkey's men who were on foot were getting mowed down. Monkey was coming around the corner in an attack truck of their own with a couple others. Abadallo jumped out of his seat, unbuckled Verdi from his seat and pulled him until he sat on the floor between the driver's seat and the passenger seat he had been in. He could see the questioning on his face so he patted him on the cheek in reassurance. He then braced the both of them as Zaccaria put the car in reverse quickly. He spun the car around and looked back to see Anna with a sniper rifle.

"How close do you need?"

"Just a little more." He kept the car in reverse and they were driving quickly towards the collection of trucks. Anna aimed carefully and hit the fuel tank of one of the attack trucks. The resulting fireball consumed both the truck and the one next to it. The third swerved away and into the arms of Monkey and his men. Monkey turned back and shouted,

"Get the hell out of here Anna!! Hope is waiting!!" Anna nodded and turned into the Humvee.

"Get us out of here Zaccaria." He put the truck in drive and they sped down the main road. Abadallo crawled into the back with Anna.

"How's our passenger?" she asked.

"He's doing alright. Still has the ear buds in and blindfold on."

"We should probably keep it that way until we're certain that we're out of danger."

"Agreed."

"Think they'll-" They heard shooting and saw another truck driving at them. It was a smaller truck. They knew they were not friends. Anna and Abadallo both pulled out their pistols and took out the tires. The truck flipped and the two people inside were flung to the road. They didn't move again.

"Answer your question?"

"Yeah." They were on the lookout for anything and everything. The fighting seemed to be concentrated in the main part of town. They heard shots, honks, shouts and a few various explosions ranging from a small firecracker to a blown gas tank. They were nearing the edge of the Terzu province and saw the various guards still in the ditches waiting to see if there was going to be a rear attack. Finally they saw the shadows of men on the roof and sending out war cries of victory. Anna let out a sigh of relief and put down the guns.

"Sleep a while back here," said Abadallo. "I'll keep Zaccaria awake."

"Sure you can?" she said with a smirk. Abadallo returned the smirk.

"I'll talk to him from the back seat." He crawled back into the middle of the truck. He pulled Verdi off the floor and put him back in the seat. Then he took the blindfold off. Verdi blinked at him for a minute and took out one of the ear buds.

"We're on our way," said Abadallo. "Feel free to sleep if you want to." Verdi nodded and tried to smile. "It's okay. I'll understand if you want to sleep with the blindfold on." Verdi nodded a little more vigorously this time and Abadallo tied the blindfold back around his head. "You doing okay Zac?"

"Yeah, doing alright." said Zaccaria. "I'll probably be good until daylight at least."

"Right. I'm going to stay back here."

"Probably best for now." Anna shut the window. She arranged the bags in the back so that she could lay down on them. Ismaele was still passed out and she put one small bag under his head. She lay down as slowly as possible to see what damage she had done to herself from the fall. After a few minutes, she was asleep.

An hour later Ismaele awoke flailing and roaring. Zaccaria was so startled he nearly ran them off the road. Abadallo drew his gun and Ismaele's flailing arm hit Anna in her already bruised ribs and brought her also roaring out of sleep and she drew on him as well.

"SHUT THE FUCK UP!" she shouted at him. He was silent. He stared at her and she stared back.

"Where are we?" he asked looking around.

"The back of the Humvee. You drank so much Monkey and I had to load you in here." He shut his eyes tight and rubbed his head.

"Is that why my skull is pounding?"

"Either that or the blows I landed on you." He looked up and saw the necklace on her neck.

"Why do you have that?" She hated this. Why did she have to do these things at the worst possible times? She put down her gun and took off the necklace.

"Teresa said to tell you, if this works and you can come back to her and be with her, you can give it back. You can be a soldier, she doesn't care." He stared at the necklace and she could see the internal pain written on his face. Abadallo moved up to the front seat and put his gun away. Ismaele didn't need more of an audience. He didn't reach for it.

"Keep it."

"Izzy-"

"Just keep it. I need to earn it back. You wear it until we come back through."

"It's not mine to wear."

"But it will be safer on you. Just wear it." She put it back on and lay back down on the bed of bags. Ismaele lay back down with a thud.

"Did she say anything else to you before we left?"

"We left in rather a hurry. Raiders were invading. Didn't leave much room for deep discussion."

"Did you say anything to her?"

"Made my feelings on her actions known."

"And those are?"

"Between me and her." There was quiet for a few minutes.

"I didn't mean-"

"I know."

"Why did I do it?"

"I don't know. Just a bad combination of everything. Don't drive yourself too crazy with it."

"She's right you know," said Verdi. They both looked up at the back of his seat. "It was a moment of crazed anger and temper. Everything that's going on right now has you on edge. You snapped for all of two seconds and stopped yourself before you did any permanent damage. In a normal world, that would have never happened." They looked at each other and then back at Verdi's seat.

"Thanks," said Ismaele slowly.

"No problem," said Verdi with a smile. The weirdest part to Abadallo was that Verdi's ear buds were still in. As far as he knew, his music was still playing. How had he heard their conversation?

Meanwhile...

The dark haired man threw the radio receiver in the back of his personal Humvee.

"Told you," said the red head. "The Terzu province is the longest standing community in this brave new world. There's a reason for that." He snarled. He reached forward and pulled her back in her seat by her hair. She half-screamed and squirmed in her seat. She reached back one hand but her grabbed her forearm before her hand reached him.

"Don't even think about it my little pet," he growled in her ear. "You need to figure out where they are going or no amount of mental trickery will save you from my wrath." He let go of her hair and she glared at him out of the corner of her eyes.

"Give me a damn map," she muttered.

# Chapter 6

Zaccaria drove until the morning light started coming up over the horizon. Abadallo took over the wheel while Zaccaria went to the back seat to sleep. From the back he heard a painful groan. Judging by the tone and timbre he guessed that it was Anna. He heard someone crawl over the back seat and fall to the floor of the truck. He looked down to see Anna's wincing face next to his seat.

"Bad morning?"

"To say the least," she whispered. "And don't shout so loud."

"Sorry," he whispered. She pulled her legs from the seat and pulled herself up into the front passenger seat. Abadallo noticed she was keeping her left arm close.

"You get hurt?"

"Yeah."

"Is it bad?"

"Not serious. Just stupidity."

"How did it happen?"

"Running up the stairs to get you guys. I tripped and fell while drunk. I know I bruised my ribs badly. Did something unspeakable to my left shoulder. Wrenched or sprained or something to it."

"Dislocated?"

"I aimed a sniper rifle last night with little trouble. Don't think it's dislocated."

"I'll take a look when we stop."

"If it makes you feel better."

"It does. So are you going to tell me what happened last night? And why you're wearing Teresa's necklace?" She didn't realize it was visible and tucked it under her shirt rather quickly.

"Ismaele... I woke up because Ismaele and Teresa were fighting again. When I got out to the landing he shouted particularly loud and I saw him with a knife to Teresa's throat. I didn't think he'd go any further but I still stopped him and sent him out. He went to the bar; I comforted and chastised Teresa, then went out and confronted him. Small fight happened and I was able to knock him out. Teresa told me to give him the necklace and tell him he can give it to her when he gets back from this and it works."

"That kind of implies that she thinks it will work."

"I know."

"She's putting far too much importance on this mission."

"I think so too. I told her so. But I doubt she heard a word I said."

"Why?"

"I don't know. Women, men, people in general, don't listen to me. They don't want to hear what I have to say."

"But you're usually right."

"I know. Many of the truths I say they don't want to hear." Abadallo nodded slowly.

"That's... very very true." She smiled regretfully at him. She knew where his mind was going.

~

A year ago she saw a problem. It was a problem with Abadallo and Zaccaria's relationship. It hadn't been that long since the mission that had nearly killed her. They were all uncertain and trying to deal with what had happened. Abadallo was tempted by a new man who had come to the base. She didn't get a good vibe off of him.

"What do you think of the new guy?" he asked her once. She hesitated. She knew she shouldn't say what she wanted to say. But to lie would be a betrayal of a trust she held dear.

"I don't like him," she said quietly. She felt more than saw Abadallo's look. She knew that look.

"Have you even given him a chance?"

"A couple. I don't like him."

"Why?"

104

"It's a vibe, okay? It's a weird oogie boogie thing I got from my grandmother. I can tell when I don't want to be around someone. He's dishonest. He likes to control and he likes to manipulate. And if you let him, he will manipulate you away from all of us."

"You just don't know him!"

"Please, just stop. You're not going to convince me to change my mind. And it looks like I'm not going to convince you to change yours. Do what you will."

It only took a day. There was a fracture. A break in their group. Abadallo was slowly being isolated from them. Zaccaria was nearly heartbroken but couldn't reach Abadallo. He tried. They all tried. But Anna had been the first to warn him. That's what he would remember when he walked in on his new almost lover in bed with someone else. He felt horrible. He felt foolish. And he realized then the rift that he had allowed to happen between him and the people he had trusted. They were eating dinner. Abadallo hadn't eaten a meal with them in a month. They were laughing and joking and sharing silly stories as always. Abadallo saw his new friend beckoning. He turned away and walked over to where his friends were sitting. They went silent when he approached. He gathered up what was left of his courage and near whispered,

"Is there room?" Anna moved her coat and patted the seat next to her.

"Sit," she said calmly. He sat. He looked across the table at Zaccaria. Zaccaria didn't look at him.

"How are you doing?" Anna asked.

"Badly," he said.

"Ah, we're being honest with each other," said Zaccaria.

"Easy," said Anna.

"No, it's fair," said Abadallo.

"You found out about the others guys, didn't you?" said Anna.

"Guys?"

"Ok, you found out about one guy?"

"Yeah..."

105

"He's a player. He plays. He manipulates. He's been going through the ranks of men around here and breaking up units."

"Why?"

"He doesn't know how to be a part of a family. And he hates those who are happy in their families. So he breaks someone away from their group, after which he dumps them. He hopes to make them as alone as he is."

"Why did he pick me?"

"You were already in the midst of a personal conflict. We all were. He saw that and took advantage." Abadallo looked across the table at Zaccaria again. Zaccaria was looking back this time.

"Do you think you guys could... take me back?" Anna looked at Ismaele and back to Abadallo.

"I think we can. It'll take some work, but I think we can. But it's not my decision alone. Boys?"

"I've committed enough sins in this life," said Ismaele. "I can give you another shot." They all turned to Zaccaria.

"Sure, we can try and fix this. Leave again and you may not be invited back." Abadallo nodded in understanding. He'd almost lost a really good thing. He wished he had listened to Anna when she said that the guy was bad news. Then he vowed that when she told him something he didn't want to hear, he would think twice.

~

Anna moved her left shoulder and winced badly. Abadallo watched her trying to move her arm.

"Ok, that's it. I'm pulling this thing over and checking you out."

"Will you respect me in the morning?" she asked with a smirk. He looked back with a serious glare. "Ok, ok, I concede to the good doctor." He slowly braked the car.

"What's happening?" said Zaccaria waking up and grabbing his gun.

"We're going to go behind the car and play doctor," said Anna.

"Oh, ok then," said Zaccaria settling back down. She reached back and slapped him awake.

"Seriously, get up. Everyone else is asleep and he's insisting on checking out my shoulder."

"Ok, ok, I'm up." All three got out of the car. Zaccaria climbed on top of the Humvee and watched all around. Abadallo had to help her out of her shirt because she couldn't lift her arm above her head. The bruises on her ribs, shoulder and arm had turned deep purple and blue.

"That really doesn't look good," said Zaccaria from above.

"You keep your mouth shut and watch the horizon," she said in annoyance. Abadallo slowly pushed her arm up until she couldn't stand it any longer.

"You might have broken it," he said. He pulled her arm gently forward and pushed it backward. She didn't like it but it wasn't as bad as trying to lift it. "I can't tell without an x-ray."

"Great."

"When you fell, how did you fall on your shoulder?"

"My full weight landed on it. My arm was tight against my side."

"Definitely not dislocation. Maybe a hairline fracture." He pulled out his medical bag and got out a sling. "Wear this whenever possible. We have to keep your arm still while the bone heals."

"I need to put a clean shirt on first." He conceded and they dug through her bag. She changed clothes and got into black pants and a black shirt. Abadallo helped her with getting dressed and then helped her with the sling. He shortened the strap until her arm was diagonally across her chest so it would stay still. Ismaele woke up as they finished this operation and blinked.

"Did I do that to you?" he asked with trepidation.

"No, did it to myself," said Anna. "Took the stairs two at a time while drunk."

"Why were you drinking last night?"

"Nothing better to do after I had to put you down. And I haven't had a good drink in a very long time. Didn't know when I would have another twenty year bottle of scotch in front of me again." Ismaele nodded.

"Ok, that's... an acceptable answer."

"Good. Considering your behavior last night, you're in no position to lecture me." She pulled the paper from last night from her sleep pants pocket and threw it at him.

"What's this?" he asked looking at it.

"The damages you caused the bar last night. You'll have to pay for it sooner or later." Ismaele looked through the list and wasn't surprised until he got to the bottom.

"A whole bottle of scotch? You guys finished a whole bottle?"

"Not the whole bottle. Rest of it is in that side compartment." Ismaele pulled open the door of the side compartment and saw the half empty bottle. "We should save it for New York." Ismaele nodded and surveyed the car.

"I may just stay back here."

"Fine by me."

"Have we had breakfast?" Abadallo and Anna looked at each other for a second and then Anna turned back.

"No, no we haven't had breakfast. We've been busy." Ismaele pulled open the food bag and found a few small cans near the top with peaches.

"Peaches all around?"

"Sure." Ismaele tossed them the cans of peaches. Abadallo tossed a can up to Zaccaria.

"Would you?" asked Anna holding out the can to Ismaele. He apologized with a look and opened the can. Anna held it in her left hand and stabbed at the peaches with a fork in her right. Ismaele tapped Verdi on the shoulder gently. Verdi turned and took off the blindfold. Ismaele saw his ear buds in so he just offered the can of peaches and a fork. Verdi smiled and accepted both items gratefully. They ate quietly for a few minutes and surveyed the land. They were still in the desert. Abadallo got out the map and continued to theorize their path.

"We should stop at Betsy's house a while. If we want to, we can stay there for lunch and a cat nap and then head on to Sun Studios."

"We started off early enough to achieve that?" said Anna with some disbelief.

"We did leave at 2:30 in the morning, you remember that right?" Anna blinked and tried to remember the events of the morning and what time they all happened.

"I guess I do. Just was concentrating on getting out."

"It's understandable." She drank the last of the juice in the can and put it away in the bag of cans they kept for trade. They each did the same and then loaded themselves back into the car. For the first time since leaving, Verdi took his headphones out of his ears.

"What's our next stop?" he asked.

"We're heading to friend's house in what's left of Oklahoma City," said Anna. "We may head on to Sun Studios after that. Be there by nightfall."

"I've never been there."

"It's mutually agreed neutral ground," said Ismaele. "Anyone who wants to stay there is safe."

"I didn't know such places existed anymore," said Verdi with surprise.

"Here and there," said Anna trying to buckle up with one hand and get comfortable. Abadallo was behind the wheel still. "Some places are just too holy to touch." Verdi smiled a strange pleased smile and put his ear buds back in.

"Is he going to wear those things all the time?" asked Abadallo.

"Keeps him happy," said Anna. Abadallo couldn't argue.

# Chapter 7

The road to Betsy's house was uneventful. Ismaele kept watch out the back for any incoming attacks. Verdi remained mostly quiet and listened to his music. At one point when all of them were awake, they started talking about old days again. Verdi took out his ear buds then and listened to them talk. He loved to listen to people talk, especially about things that made them happy. Currently they were talking about their favorite lunches.

"Open-faced tuna melt sandwich with tomato on a salt bagel," said Anna. The others expressed their appreciation as she imagined it so vividly that she could almost taste it. "God I loved having one of those on summer day. Was always so good sitting on a bench in central park."

"I loved to get a slice or two around the corner from the insurance company," said Zaccaria. "Always good pizza."

"The base hired little old ladies to cook," said Ismaele. "Little old Italian ladies who created incredible food out of nothing. I rarely ate off base. Everything they made was good."

"Hot dog stand," said Abadallo.

"What a surprise," said Anna with a smirk.

"They were convenient."

"I'm sure they were." Verdi looked around and saw they were driving down a long road and was almost completely devoid of scenery. There was an occasional ruin of a building here and there. But signs of life were nowhere to be seen.

"What about you Verdi?" said Anna.

"I'm sorry, what was the question?" he said snapping out of his daze.

"What did you like to get best for lunch? In the old days?"

"Oh, you'll think I'm silly."

"Sillier than hotdogs?" said Abadallo with a grin.

"Waffle House, pecan waffle with a side of bacon."

"Oh Lord that would be fantastic right about now," said Anna with a groan.

"I know, man that place was so bad for you but so good late at night or early in the morning or anytime you were drunk," said Ismaele thinking about the last time he had anything from a Waffle House.

"I take it you went to several Waffle Houses in your day then," said Abadallo with a playful shove.

"Oh yes," said Ismaele with a grin.

"Why would we think that was silly?" asked Anna.

"You were all talking about really nice and unique places."

"It's not about that. It's about your memory. Lots of places are just common every day places to most people. For some, that place can be the holiest of holies."

"Hold on everyone," said Abadallo. "This is going to get a little bumpy." He turned off down a road that was broken and rough. He dodged the various barricades that were set up to hide Betsy's house. One last turn around a barrier and they were at a blue and purple house at the end of the street. Betsy came out of the house in a long summer dress with a shawl around her shoulders. Anna jumped out of the Humvee and the two long-time friends ran to each other and embraced warmly.

"God I was so scared about you when I heard," Betsy said close to her ear.

"I know, I know honey," she said holding her friend tight. "It's okay, we're okay."

"How long are you staying?"

"Only a couple of hours. We don't want to stay long and lead the raiders that have been following us here." They two finally pulled back from each other. "Snake still here?"

"Yeah, he's got his eye in the sky still going. You can check with him."

"Good." She turned back and saw the others slowly getting out of the Humvee. Verdi had retreated back into his

112

headphones and blindfold.  Zaccaria and Abadallo were easily leading him out and towards the house.

"Is that...?"

"The hope of the future?  Yeah, that's him."  Betsy looked at him and then back at Anna.  "I know, I thought the same exact thoughts you are thinking."

"Why are you on this mission?"

"Because something has to happen at some point.  We can't just keep going like we have been."  Betsy nodded and turned back to the house.  Betsy had long blond hair that she kept up in a tight bun on the back of her head.  Her eyes were a bright blue and she was always very thin.  She was also nearly six feet tall.  She led them into the dim rooms of her house.  They took Verdi into the parlor and put him in a quiet corner so he wouldn't be disturbed.  Abadallo sat down to keep an eye on him.  Anna went downstairs into the basement with Betsy to talk to Snake.

The stairs to the basement were narrow, dark and they creaked with every step.  Betsy knocked on the door at the bottom of the stairs.

"Yeah?" shouted a man's voice with a thick country accent.

"Visitors," she shouted back.

"Visitors we want to see?"

"Visitors we thought we'd never see again."  There was a creaking of chair springs and the sound of boots on wood floor and the door opened.  Snake was the same height as Anna.  He kept his ash blond hair closely cropped and his eyes were grey.  He wasn't muscular but he wasn't skinny.  His body was always well-toned.  He squinted for a moment to see who was behind Betsy but then his eyes went wide.  He ran forward and pounced on Anna bringing her down hard on the stairs.

"Oh my God we thought you were goners!!"

"Easy Snake!!  Easy, the shoulder isn't doing well!" she said with a giggle.  He pulled back and saw her arm in the sling.

"What did you do?"

"Would you believe all I did was fall?"  He looked at her suspiciously.

"Did you really just fall?"

"I really did just fall."

"How bad is it?"

"Abadallo thinks it's broken. Can't say for certain."

"Well, I finally got the x-ray machine going, so I can tell you for certain."

"That would be fantastic, but first I need you to use your eye in the sky for something important."

"Whatcha need?"

"Raiders have been following us. Monkey took out most, possibly all. I need you to take a look and see if there are any raiders coming here."

"You got it. This will take me a few minutes so let's fire up that x-ray machine and see what you've done to your shoulder." Snake led them over to another part of the basement where there was an old x-ray machine sitting in a corner. He turned on the light to position the image correctly. She slowly stretched out her arm and he took the picture. He repositioned her in all the annoying ways that doctors did and finally he put the pictures up on the light. He looked at them carefully and muttered to himself.

"Has he always acted like this?" she asked Betsy.

"Only when he's playing doctor," she replied.

"You didn't seem to mind it last night," he said over his shoulder to Betsy. Betsy smiled and blushed. Anna chuckled. "If you had landed any harder you probably would have cracked it completely," he said studying one of the x-rays. "But as is it looks like you only badly bruised it. I'd still give it a rest whenever possible in that sling. But there's no dislocation and no complete break. You should be good in a week or so."

"Thanks Snake."

"No problem. My equipment probably still needs some more time so go on upstairs and get comfy." She and Betsy went back up the stairs and into the kitchen.

Ismaele and Zaccaria were in the dining room taking stock. They hadn't since they had been at Shakespeare's house and they weren't sure when they would be able to get supplies again after this house. Sun Studios usually had stock of needed things, but there was no telling how many had been though. They laid

114

out the guns first with the ammunition for each. The explosives came next. Then the knives and various hand to hand weapons that they had lying about or on their person. On the other half of the table they lined up the food and water that they still had. Once done they stepped back and surveyed their collection.

"So, we have more in weapons and ammunition than food," said Zaccaria.

"We're a five man crew, we really don't need that much in food," said Ismaele. "And raiders are more my concern."

Zaccaria nodded looking over their haul. "Still, we probably should get some more food before we leave here. Never know when we'll be able to pick up some more again. How are we doing on gas?"

"We still have three five gallon tanks in the back."

"Right, probably should get some more."

"So, ammunition, soup, fruit, water and gas."

"Yeah, that looks to be all we need." Zaccaria looked back towards the kitchen.

"Should I go in there-"

"No, don't. This might be the last time they see each other. They'll want to talk."

Anna and Betsy knew each other from before. They were in the orchestra together. They both played the cello. Betsy had sat next to her for years. They had the bond of musicians.

"What's your name this time?" said Betsy as she brewed the tea. Anna finally allowed herself to laugh cynically for nearly a full minute before answering.

"Anna," she replied looking at Betsy. Her longtime friend turned and stared at her in shock.

"You're joking," she said in an astounded tone.

"Nope, wish that I were."

"Who had that great idea?"

"Our target, Verdi. He wanted code names he could remember."

"Where did he get the names from?"

"Verdi's "Nabucco"."

115

"That's... weirdly appropriate to our current situation."

"I nearly fell out of my chair when they told us our code names."

"So what's this guy's great plan?"

"I have no idea. If he tells someone, he swears them to secrecy. He won't tell any of us. He doesn't want us to keep secrets from each other."

"He's smarter than the others."

"That he's already proven a few times over. But there is one major drawback."

"What's that?"

"He's agoraphobic." Betsy steeped the tea and placed an empty cup in front of Anna.

"How did you get him here?"

"A blindfold and an iPod can do wonders when trying to get an agoraphobe out the door and into a waiting vehicle."

"Has he taken those off at all since you got him in the Humvee?"

"A couple of times. He actually engaged in conversation with us before we got here. Guess it was the idea of going from the Humvee to the house that scared him back into his hole. And last night..." She began to seriously think about last night. He hadn't taken the ear buds out. But he had heard them.

"Last night what?" said Betsy pouring the tea.

"I don't know, last night he said something to Ismaele. Something he needed to hear. But I don't know how he heard us discussing it. He still had his ear buds in."

"Was the music on?"

"I... don't know."

"Maybe that's how he heard. I know I can hear everyone around me if I have ear buds in and no music playing. Maybe he just didn't want to be disturbed."

"Maybe. I don't know. There's something weird about this guy."

"Weird bad?"

"I'm not getting a weird bad vibe. Just a weird vibe."

"Hate to break it to you babe but you're not that normal yourself." Anna stuck her tongue out at her friend and Betsy just chuckled.

"You're one to talk."

"Hey, I was your second. I took care of you and kept you grounded!"

"And challenged me to several drinking games while in public."

"Ok, I'll give you that one."

"What did you do in the bet?"

"Alright!" said Betsy playfully shoving Anna. "I said that's enough!" Anna sipped her tea and she felt good again.

"How is it you know how to make tea to suit every situation?" she asked for the millionth time in their friendship.

"I know you," said Betsy with a kind smile. They both heard footsteps running up the stairs and a breathless Snake swung through the open door.

"Anna, you have to see this," he said with an edge in his voice.

"What is it?" she asked nervously.

"Something I really don't want to show you, but I have to." Anna slowly stood on shaking knees and walked with Snake and Betsy down the steps to his computers. He had a picture up on the screen. He didn't have to tell her what it was. She already knew.

"No, no no no not him!" she shouted at the screen feeling the tears welling up in her eyes unbidden. It was Shakespeare's house. It was in fire and ruin.

"I was trying to call him, to see what he might have heard. This is all I got back." He pushed a button and they heard an automated message. They just barely recognized Shakespeare's voice.

"This is the Globe Theater to all the ships at sea. We've been compromised. Not sure how much longer this place will remain standing. Tried to keep the secrets as best we could. Assume all information known. I have no idea what the others said. To Isolated Incident and the rest of the crew, keep going, hope is waiting." Snake pushed the button and the message stopped.

"Who's Isolated Incident?" asked Betsy.

"That's me," said Anna. "He called me that because I'm an only child." Anna turned around and curled into a ball in the big easy chair Snake kept in the corner. Betsy curled around her and held her while she cried.

Meanwhile...

The red head was staring at the map spread out on the seat. The dark haired man was cleaning his gun in the other seat. She tried to clear her head and listen clearly. But the clicks and snaps from his activity kept distracting.

"If you could stop that for five minutes-" she said but then looked him in the eye. He was not about to stop. She looked down at the map again with an angry sigh. She followed the roads with her eyes until one felt right. He never could hide from her for very long. "They're in Oklahoma City now."

"You mean what's left of Oklahoma City." She rolled her eyes and glared at him.

"They're in **what's left** of Oklahoma City."

"We won't be able to reach them before they make the next leg on their journey."

"I highly doubt it."

"Then you'll just have to work harder and keep an eye on them. Won't you?" She folded up the map and handed it back to the driver and navigator.

"Head for what's left of Oklahoma City. We'll see where they are headed next soon enough."

## Chapter 8

Meanwhile, Verdi was in the parlor slowly taking off his blindfold. The first thing he saw was Abadallo calmly cleaning his gun. Taken into pieces, it looked more like an infinitely crazy puzzle rather than a weapon of destruction and death. Abadallo was systematically cleaning and oiling the parts of the gun and slowly piecing it back together again.

"Why are you doing that?" asked Verdi.

"Helps me think," said Abadallo without looking up.

"How?"

"It helps me to organize my thoughts and envision the road ahead of me. That way I can make sure it all comes together properly." Two large pieces slid together evenly and finished with a click.

"I don't know how you stand those things."

"It took some time."

~

Abadallo remembered when he first started as a soldier. Zaccaria was the one who had taught him how to shoot long ago when they were boys with B. B. guns. Now they were shooting stuff far more powerful. The others were trying to force bigger guns into his hands and would tell him to just aim and hold on. He just couldn't get his aim right with the bigger ones. He was better at the small guns and his aim was far more accurate. Zaccaria came down to the firing range and saw him working with a pistol while the others sniggered.

"What's your problem?" asked Zaccaria to the others.

"Ain't no one is going to be afraid of this pussy and his tiny little gun!" said one of them. The others guffawed and chuckled loudly. Zaccaria could see Abadallo's ears turn red.

"I wouldn't be so dismissive if I were you," said Zaccaria. He knew better than to mess with Abadallo with a pistol in his hands. He was good.

"What's this guy gonna do?" said a second. "Give us a paper cut."

"No, but he could shoot off your balls if you're not careful." The blush left Abadallo's ears. Zaccaria stood in the stand next to him. He knew that what was about to happen. Probably wasn't the best of ideas, but it would get them to shut up.

"Him? He couldn't-" Then there were three shots. Only three. Abadallo had turned towards the jokers, took aim and shot three times. The one on the right lost a button off his jacket cuff. The one on the left lost half a shoelace. And the one in the middle lost the hammer strap off the side of his pants. They were all stunned into silence. This had all occurred in a second. They looked at themselves and each other to determine if there was any serious injury and then found the bits they had lost at their feet.

"Damn..." whispered the ringleader of this trio in obvious admiration. They looked up at him. Abadallo smiled, winked and then turned back to continue his target practice. The three finding that they were quite embarrassed turned away and walked out of the gun range. Only Zaccaria and Abadallo were left on the range. During a pause Abadallo said,

"Do you think I'll get in trouble for that little stunt?" There was a confidence back in his voice that Zaccaria hadn't heard since the day the world went nuts. It made him smile just to hear it.

"I doubt it. Technically they weren't hurt and I seriously doubt they would like to recount their tale of shame to anyone."

"Good." Abadallo stepped around the wall that separated them and Zaccaria put his gun down. They had been sleeping in the same bed for a month. Both were still full of raw nerves and in mourning for the losses they had faced. And maybe that was why it was so easy for Abadallo to reach up, touch Zaccaria's face and lean in to kiss him gently on the lips. They had kissed like this once before. Years ago when they were fumbling stumbling teenagers on a hot summer night out camping. Back then they were new explorers on a whirlwind track to who knew where. They had the whole night and they didn't sleep until they had mapped out every inch of each other and explored all that one could dare to when time was of the essence and adults were nearby sleeping in their own tents. Zaccaria had been the one then to cross the lines and kiss Abadallo. Now Zaccaria was kissing back and pulling his friend near. They broke the kiss at the same time when they heard someone coming. Zaccaria looked around the partition and saw another man just passing by the open range. He didn't seem to see them. He turned back to his friend and kissed him gently.

"We should continue this elsewhere," said Zaccaria quietly. "If you want to."

"I do," said Abadallo. "I just..."

"I know." It was hard for the both of them. That night they kissed and cuddled and whispered about time and pain and life. Life was too short now to process anything properly. At least that was the way it seemed. So they were together, for now. If things didn't work out, either could cut loose without much damage done. And that was the way it went and the way it was still going.

~

"He loves you," said Verdi suddenly. Abadallo looked up from his gun with a slow turn.

"Who?"

"Zaccaria," said Verdi with a look of disbelief.

"Oh," said Abadallo looking down at his gun again.

"He loves you," Verdi repeated.

"We don't say such things."

"Why not?" said Verdi in an exasperated tone. "You know. He knows. Everyone around you knows unless they are deaf and blind."

"I don't care about Anna and Ismaele knowing. They'll protect us to their last drop of blood. People might be listening."

"People don't have to be listening to see it." Abadallo looked up at Verdi.

"How do you know these things?" Verdi suddenly looked uncomfortable and seemed to shrink into his chair.

"I just... I'm just observant."

"No, this isn't just being observant. Zaccaria said you asked him about the two of us. He didn't say much, but by the look on your face and the way you hugged him, he swore that you knew more. Like you knew what he was thinking of. And last night you had your music on the whole time didn't you? How did you hear Ismaele and Anna talking? And how did you know what to say to him?"

"It was between songs. I just heard what he said." Verdi was closing his eyes tight trying to shut out the panic.

"No you didn't. There's only three seconds between songs on an iPod like yours. Three seconds isn't enough time to hear what they said."

"They were quiet songs."

"I didn't say that out loud." Verdi's eyes snapped open and he saw Abadallo sitting three inches away from him. "You're telepathic, aren't you?"

"I... just..."

"Don't. Are you telepathic? Can you hear me thinking right now?" Verdi let out a long sigh and felt like he was deflating. Half the tension in his body left and he slumped forward slightly.

"Yes," he whispered. "That's why the headphones. When I put them on and turn on the music I can drown out most of the voices."

"And the agoraphobia?"

"Mostly a product of that. I don't like going out where there are lots of people. It gets too loud and noisy. I can barely breathe or see straight or even think. Sometimes I've even fainted."

"But somewhere like here?"

"Six people in the house total. A little spread out, I can deal easily. If someone gets too angry or loud then I can just put in the headphones again. Or else retreat to some quiet room away from everyone." Abadallo looked up at him with trepidation.

"You know my real name, don't you?"

"Yes."

"You know all our real names."

"I know the real names of every single person I've traveled with and I've never told a soul."

"Good God I thought Shakespeare was a bomb waiting to happen. You're a fucking nuclear weapon!!"

"I swear Abadallo; I swear I won't tell anyone. I've never told anyone anything!!"

"How many have traveled with you over the years?"

"I have no idea."

"How many?!" Verdi could feel the others being alerted by Abadallo's voice. They wouldn't be alone for much longer.

"Dozens, hundreds, I have no idea how many."

"How many are still alive?"

"What?!" Anna came to the door and peered in.

"What seems to be the problem in here?" Verdi saw her red eyes and her tear-streaked cheeks and knew she wasn't going to help.

"How many are still alive?!"

"I don't know Abadallo! I don't know!!! I move from place to place so much that I never can tell who is still around and who's not!"

"Hey!" shouted Anna walking into the room and laying a hand on Abadallo's shoulder. "What seems to be the problem here?"

"He's telepathic!" said Abadallo pointing at Verdi. "He can read our thoughts! I bet he can even sense our memories!"

"What?"

"What's all the commotion?" said Ismaele appearing at the door with Zaccaria. Verdi clapped his hands down over his ears, shut his eyes tight and tried to hum to himself to keep out the noise. Abadallo was angry. Anna was upset, confused and on her way to angry and the other two were irritated and confused. It was all too much at the moment in a group that had been very serene and calming to be around. Now they were a jumble. Abadallo was shouting at the others and still pointing. Zaccaria was getting angry as well. Anna had gone quickly past anger and into rage. Something had upset her and this new discovery was

125

only adding fuel to the fire. There was only one person in the room not shouting and remarkably remaining calm: Ismaele. He stepped into the room and shouted above the others. They fell into line quickly. They were still angry, but they were quiet. Verdi looked up and Ismaele was gesturing to Verdi and giving them an admonishing look. The other three left the room and went elsewhere in the house. He couldn't hear them anymore. Ismaele sat down in front of him in the chair Abadallo had been sitting in. He stopped humming. He could hear Ismaele thinking,

"Whenever you're ready kid, I'm just here to listen and understand." Verdi slowly took his hands off his ears. "Music calms you?" said Ismaele out loud.

"Yes," said Verdi straightening a little. "And it shuts out the voices and feelings I don't want in my head... sometimes."

"One or two or four can be shut out, but I'm guessing in a room of a hundred it would be impossible."

"Yes."

"How long have you... How long have you known you were telepathic?"

"Always. I used to listen to my mother's thoughts when I was a child and she would hold me. She loved me entirely. Then I would hear Dad thinking about the woman he was banging across town."

"Yikes."

"Yeah. I told her at some point. She thought I was making things up. Dad nearly beat me to death. She didn't think I was making things up anymore after that."

"How old were you?"

"I think I was... five? Maybe four? Just slipped out one day. I asked if I was ever going to meet daddy's lady across town."

"What did your mom do?"

"Divorced him. Moved us out into the country. I liked it out there. It was quieter out there."

"Us?"

"I have a twin sister."

"Is she telepathic as well?"

126

"Yes."

"Where is she?"

"I have no idea. I really truly have no idea. We haven't spoken in fifteen years. Had a kind of... falling out I guess you could say." In that moment, Ismaele could see the pain written all over Verdi's face.

"I'm sorry."

"Me too."

"I'm also sorry for how the others reacted. You have to understand, we've all been on the run the last three years."

"And you think I haven't?" Ismaele sighed and kept his anger in check.

"You've been protected, yes?" Verdi saw his point.

"I have been. Very well protected."

"We've been on our own. Survival instincts, you see. We get brutal even with each other at times. They'll calm down in a little while. I have to ask you certain questions that they want answered. Once I give them the answers, they'll probably chill out. Do you understand?"

"Yes."

"Okay. Do you know our real names?"

"Yes."

"Are you going to sell that information to anyone to track us?"

"No."

"Have you ever sold that kind of information to raiders to track others?"

"No."

"Are your past protectors still alive?"

"As far as I know only one is dead. He died from a spear through the chest when the group I was with was making a very narrow escape. If others are dead I don't know about it and I don't know how. I hope they are all alive."

"How much do you know about us?" All the other answers Verdi had been immediately forthcoming. On this question he faltered. He wasn't sure how much he should say. "Verdi? I really need an answer to this one. They're worried. They're exposed in a time when being exposed is an extreme liability. They want to know."

"I know... much. If you've thought about it since being around me, I know it."

"Give me something specific."

"I know how angry Zaccaria felt when he sliced up the men who raped Abadallo. I know how Abadallo felt when he finally got up the courage to kiss Zaccaria at the gun range. I know something is wrong with Anna. I don't know what it is but it has her extremely upset and in a rage. And I know how crazy it's driving you that you might be more like your father than you want to be." Ismaele's expression flashed to anger in a second but Verdi sat still. "You're not. You're not him. I told you that last night." Ismaele's expression calmed again.

"Do you intend to use that information against any of us?"

"No. Never. And I have never used any information I've ever learned about anyone against them."

"Stay in here for now. Do whatever you need to do to remain calm. I'll talk to them." He slowly walked to the door and turned back for a second.

"You're wondering whether or not you believe in telepathy," said Verdi looking down at the carpet.

"Yeah..."

"When the four of you fight, you fight as one. It's always been that way. You're not telepaths, your brainwaves just fit together. It happens more often than you think. Some people just fit together. I've seen it a lot. And some just clash like train wrecks. So you hear each other. Not the way I hear you, but you still hear each other."

"It's useful."

"It's gotten the four of you out of a lot of scrapes."

"Yes..."

"Yes, you and your wife fit together. Very well as a matter of fact."

"Teresa?"

"You have bumps. It's not a perfect fit, but I've seen some of the best relationships come out of an imperfect fit. Don't sign

128

her off just yet." Ismaele turned back and walked out the door. He quietly shut it behind him. He stood there for a minute trying to process everything he had just heard. He knew the others were about. He knew they wanted answers. He pulled himself up straight and shouted so it could be heard throughout the house.

"Oi! All of you! Front porch! Now!" The parlor was near the back of the house. The front porch a good distance away. He estimated that they would be able to talk and not disturb Verdi too much. He walked up the hallway and heard the others scrambling from their various hideaways and quickly making their way to the porch. He walked out to the three of them standing at attention.

"Sit!" he said. They all sat down in the chairs on the porch. "Now, before I go on. Going off half-cocked on the man that may hold the key to our salvation, for any reason, is a bad idea. Do it again, and you're off this team. Do I make myself clear?" There was indignant silence. He snapped into drill sergeant mode again for a moment and shouted, "I said, DO I MAKE MYSELF CLEAR?!"

"Yes, sir!" they shouted. Even though they were sitting, they snapped up straight in their seats.

"Now, I have spoken to him. I have asked him certain questions. He gave me the answers to those questions and I believe them to be truthful answers. You will listen to them now whether you like it or not. Yes, he is telepathic. Yes, he knows our real names. Yes, he knows a good deal about all of us. If you have thought about it in his presence in the past few days, he has probably heard it. He told me a few of the things he has heard. They are very personal and close things that we all know about each other but others don't necessarily know about us. Some of these things could be used against us were others to find them out. However, he has no intention or plan to use any of this information against us. Furthermore, of the people who have protected him, he only knows of one fatality. I believe if he were working for raiders, he would be keeping track of all his confirmed kills. He really truly wishes us and others no ill will. Now, does anyone have a problem?" The others were silent for a moment. But he could hear them thinking. He remembered what Verdi

129

said. Their brain waves simply fit together. With every passing second, he was certain Verdi was right. "I can hear the cogs turning in your heads, what is the question of the day?"

"How can we be sure?" said Abadallo.

"I'm sure we can be sure because every answer he gave me was immediate and truthful. His only hesitation was telling me how much he had heard from us."

"Why was he spying on us like that?"

"He wasn't spying. It's not an active thing. We were close by. And he heard."

"Can he hear us now?" said Anna with an edge in her voice. Verdi was right again. Something had happened that was bothering her.

"No. He seems to have a limit on how far he can hear. I think he's thankful for it. He knows we're in the house. He just can't hear us."

"Has anyone thought to ask him what his great idea is yet?" said Zaccaria. The others looked at each other.

"Do we want to know?" said Anna in a cynical voice.

"What if it's mind control?" asked Abadallo.

"It's not," said Verdi from the door to the house. "I can hear what you're thinking. I can't control your thoughts even if I tried."

"What is your plan?" said Ismaele.

"Is that an order?"

"No, a request."

"I'll tell you when we get closer to New York."

"Do you think we won't take you if we know?" said Abadallo.

"I'm not sure that you would." Anna launched out of her chair and walked straight up to Verdi and looked him in the eye.

"We've taken many across the country with the knowledge that it might not work," said Anna. "A few we were even certain before we left that it wouldn't work. What makes yours so special?"

"It might."

"Did you tell them where to find Shakespeare?"

"What?" he said now completely confused.

"Did you tell them where to find Shakespeare and don't make out like you don't know who he is! If you've heard our thoughts this whole time you know he's the man I'm in love with! The man I'm in love with who is now dead!" The others looked at her in shock. Betsy appeared at the door with a worried look on her face. "Did you tell them where to find Shakespeare?!"

"I didn't Anna!" he shouted back. "I heard you think about him but none of you ever thought of his location until now. I wouldn't have been able to do it if I wanted to and I never want to!" Anna was trying hard not to break into pieces and he could see that. He tried to reach for her but she backed away instantly.

"Don't touch me!" she shouted at him. Betsy ran past him and grabbed her hands.

"It's alright Anna, he doesn't mean any harm," she said to her reassuringly.

"How do you know that?" she half shouted half wailed. "How do you know?"

"You know me Anna; you've known me for years. You and I have always been able to tell about people. You and I both know he's a good man." Anna was wrapped In Betsy's arms again and she looked at him regretfully. He nodded slowly and retreated back into the house slowly. The others looked at each other.

"We have a mission," said Ismaele reminding them why they were there. "The Captain ordered us on this mission. It was his last order." Abadallo's eyes suddenly went wide with realization. "What?"

"That's it... it wasn't Verdi. That's how the raiders knew where we were!"

"What?"

"They raided home. They saw Captain's plans. One of his suggested routes was the one I picked! They must have just sent a few scouts and started following the damn map, oh my God I've been so stupid!!"

"Ok, it's ok. Hopefully we've shook them. Has anyone checked with Snake yet?"

"No, I need to go do that," said Anna pulling away from Betsy. She went back into the house with Betsy close behind.

"Abadallo, you need to start to think of an alternate plan than the one we've got."

"Right, I'll get right on that."

"Get your rifle first." Abadallo nodded and turned into the house.

"Zac, you and I need to finish the inventory and planning. This could get interesting." Abadallo walked back into the parlor. Verdi was there listening to his iPod. Abadallo was only there to get his gun and sat back down to finish putting it together. He was almost done when Verdi said,

"You don't have to keep apologizing." Abadallo looked up at him. "I've gotten far worse from far more evil men than you."

"I'm sorry-"

"I said, stop apologizing. I get it. You were protecting yourself and you were protecting those around you. I understand."

"We're getting some information from Snake so we know where would be safe to stay tonight."

"We're not going to Sun Studios?"

"We may still. It is still recognized neutral ground."

"Why?"

"It's kind of like holy ground. Old rules. No fighting on holy ground. It's disrespectful." He snapped his sniper rifle together and went down in the basement to meet with Snake and Anna. They were both looking with concerned expressions at a large digital map on the wall.

"What's the word?" asked Abadallo.

"Not good," said Snake. "You were thinking of heading to Atlanta?"

"Yeah, good drop point-"

"Not anymore. There's a high concentration of raiders there. Any state below Tennessee is no place to be right now."

"That... that means we won't be able to find cover from Memphis to..."

"Washington, DC," said Anna. "I know, but there isn't any other way around it."

"The place is... it's toxic. Isn't it?"

"Only if you decide to set up camp there for a month," said Snake. "One night, just one night, you should be able to get out without too many ill effects. But you are heading up to New York. That's like walking into the lion's den."

"And waking the dragon," said Anna. "New York... it's..."

"It's where we're going," said Abadallo. "And I'm going to make sure that we can get in." Anna raised an eyebrow and followed him out of the basement.

"You've certainly changed your tune quickly."

"I thought he was leading the raiders here. I was wrong."

"And that was why you were angry?"

"That was the majority of it, yes. Why? You angry with him for some other reason?"

"He kept what he was from us."

"With good reason, look how we all reacted! We all say that we would follow and do whatever had to be done but look at us!! We immediately got suspicious and jumped all over him. If many people know what he is... you know how people would react. And you know he would be hunted."

"He is being hunted."

"We have to protect him. We have to protect him until we reach New York. Then he will do... whatever it is that he is going to do."

"It better be something spectacular or I'm going to be really pissed." Anna walked into the parlor and saw Verdi listening to his iPod again.

"We're getting ready to leave," she said calmly. He looked up and nodded. She walked into the room and helped him tie on his blindfold. He touched her hand gently and said,

"If it makes you feel any better, I will be really pissed with myself if this doesn't work." She took off his blindfold and looked him in the eye. She motioned for him to take out the ear buds and he did.

"Do you think this will work?"

133

"Yes. I think it will."

"And if it doesn't?"

"It's completely my fault." She nodded and motioned to him to put his ear buds back in. She tied on his blindfold and gently led him back out to the Humvee. Ismaele and Zaccaria were loading up the back of the vehicle. Once it was all organized like they wanted, Ismaele climbed into the back and Zaccaria shut him in. Anna got Verdi strapped into his seat and then sat in the driver's seat. Abadallo sat next to her and Zaccaria climbed in the backseat. Before they started the car, Betsy ran out to the car with a package in her hands.

"This is for you all, for the road."

"Thanks Betsy," Anna said with a smile. She could tell by the size and shape that the package was full of cookies. The two blew kisses to each other and then Anna turned on the car.

"Come back to me," Betsy said with a sad smile. Anna returned the expression and replied,

"If it's written in the stars my love, I will." They drove off in the direction of Memphis.

Meanwhile…

The red head was dozing in the back seat of the Humvee. While sleeping she could track him better. Sometimes if they were both asleep she could slip in and watch his dreams. Right now he was dozing in another vehicle. He was listening to classical music again. She heard a voice talking and tried to listen. But he turned up the volume on his music so she couldn't hear anything. She opened her eyes and looked at the dark haired man.

"They're heading to Memphis. That was all I could catch before he shut me out."

"Does he suspect?"

"I don't think so. I think he just wants to be left alone."

"Then why is he doing this?"

"He doesn't have anything else."

# Chapter 9

Their journey from Oklahoma City to Memphis was also
mostly uneventful. And Anna was thankful for that. Most of the
time the boys slept. She hummed gently to herself and tried to
keep her mind focused on the road ahead. It had been a while
since she had been in Memphis. She knew the place was going
to be nothing like the way she left it. It made her apprehensive
about approaching the place again. Places she had never seen
before the world went nuts didn't bother her. She didn't know
what it was supposed to look like. Memphis was where she had
grown up. Where she danced her first steps. Where she got her
first kiss. Memphis was important on so many levels. They were
getting close as night started to fall. She looked ahead and
couldn't see the sky line. She had been told that Graceland and
Sun Studios still stood. No one had the heart to bring the places
down. No one was that cruel. But she remembered buildings and
places that didn't exist anymore. They got to the edge of town
and she slowed to a stop. Abadallo woke up next to her and
looked out.

"What's going on?" he asked looking around for her reason
for stopping. She didn't reply. He looked over and saw the tears
in her eyes. "Been a while?" He remembered that Memphis was
where she was born and grew up. They had been dozens of
places all around the country but they had rarely come back here.
She nodded. He reached over and squeezed her shoulder. "We
can wake one of the others if you want to." She shook her head
and wiped the tears away from her eyes.

"No, I'm good. Let's just go." She put the car in drive
again and rolled forward. Buildings were blown out. Glass and
wreckage everywhere. She got off the interstate and onto Union

Ave. Sun Studio was ahead. She pulled in and parked behind the building.

"Wake up everyone," she said to the others. "Put your shoes on, we're at grandma's." There was a light chuckle through the car as they slowly pulled their tired limbs out of their seats and walked to the back door. Anna knocked on the door and waited for a minute. The door opened and a man with raven black hair and blue eyes opened the door.

"Hey there blackbird!" he said with a smile.

"Hey there Elvis," she said in reply and returned his smile with a tired one. "Any room at the inn?"

"Sugar you always know we have room, come on in and rest your tired bones." Zaccaria and Ismaele pulled Verdi from the vehicle and led him blindly into the building. It was crowded. It was always crowded. Ismaele could feel Verdi shaking. He reached into Verdi's pocket and pulled out the perpetually playing iPod. He saw the charge was getting low and they would need to fix that soon. For now he put the volume on loud and chose a symphony. Verdi started at first but then squeezed his hand in thanks. Ismaele led him to the quietest and least populated room he could find and sat him down. He took his hand and said to him in his mind,

"Just stay here a little while kid. We'll see where we're sleeping tonight. Maybe we can find somewhere quieter." Verdi nodded and squeezed Ismaele's hand. Ismaele patted him on the arm and then stood up. He looked around the room and saw a couple of vaguely familiar faces. They nodded in friendly recognition. He nodded back. He and Zaccaria walked back through the crowded hallway and into the room where Anna and Abadallo were. They were looking at the guest book and determining where they could stay that night. Sometimes people stayed there. It was neutral territory and no one was allowed to cause trouble or else be kicked out in the middle of the night. Anna turned as they entered the room.

"We just might be staying in Graceland tonight."

"Cool," said Ismaele with a smile. "We need to find a quiet place for Verdi tonight. This place is really messing with his state

138

of mind." Anna looked about and realized then how crowded the place was. Crowded rooms were the norm these days. She hardly ever thought about it anymore.

"Then our plan may work," said Elvis. "You guys are on an important mission and you need to be highly protected. Best place for that to happen is Graceland. Guarded well, gates, codes, the works. And anything you want charged can be charged up there."

"How do we get in?"

"You have to sing."

They all piled into the front room to the famous microphone that everyone had sung into. They would sing to determine who got to sleep in Graceland that night. They had a few iPods and a karaoke machine that still worked most nights. Even if it was a competition, it was still really fun. That's why everyone was piled in as closely as possible in the room. Cigarettes, beer and anticipation filled the air. The first few were okay. It was mostly fun to watch them crash and burn. Most everyone expected to sleep shoulder to shoulder on the floor anyway. So the first few were not serious competitors. A blond guy without a tune in his body since the day he was born tried to stumble his way through Wang Chung's "Everybody Have Fun Tonight". He forgot some of the words and muttered a bunch. Next was another guy who tried to scream his way through "Back in Black" by AC/DC. He didn't have a tune in his body but he sang with such abandon that he had the crowd cheering for him and jamming with him. Anna got up to sing now and she had chosen Bon Jovi's "Dead or Alive". She could sing better than her competitors and she had the whole crowd singing the response to her shout of "Wanted!" and joining in with her for "dead or alive". She wasn't a singer. But she loved to sing this song. Another competitor got up and gave an incredible performance of The Who's "Pinball Wizard". They had competition. Zaccaria then sang a blistering rendition of The Who's "Reign O'er Me". The race was close. The next one of the other team sang a good round of "Everlong" by Foo Fighters. They just needed a deal closer. That was when Verdi appeared at the door. His protectors all looked at him warily. He walked to

Elvis and whispered in his ear. Elvis nodded and Verdi motioned to the four of them. Anna walked to him and whispered,

"What are you up to?"

"A deal closer," he said with a smirk and a wink. She looked at the song queuing up and she laughed out loud. The others saw what she saw and nearly died of laughter. But they stood behind him as backup singers and got themselves ready. They sang the first notes of "Bohemian Rhapsody" and room finally got the joke. They all laughed as well until Verdi began to sing by himself. His voice was incredible. He sang with perfect pitch. And everyone in the room couldn't take their eyes away. Hilarity and excitement took over as the quicker section started and the others sang their back up parts in perfect operatic style. The room bounced and smiled and laughed and the raucous guitar and drum part threatened to shake the building apart as they danced and stomped around. At last all that was left was Verdi singing gently and the others singing the last few notes. The crowd applauded for three minutes. They were the clear winners. They were celebrating and laughing and almost forgot how uncomfortable Verdi was until he reached for Ismaele's elbow and squeezed it hard. Ismaele turned and nodded. Elvis started into a gentle version of "Danny Boy" which was every night's closer. People calmed and settled. Several took the hint and retreated to their rooms. Ismaele stayed tight beside Verdi.

"We'll be out of here soon," he whispered to the timid man beside him. "The others really like this song. Let them have their moment of sorrow." Verdi nodded and tried to smile. "Have your iPod still?"

"I really like this song." Ismaele nodded in understanding. Everyone loved this song. Especially the way Elvis sang it. His voice was like a soothing balm to all the wounds everyone in the building had collected over the last three years.

They all piled back into the Humvee and headed for Graceland. At the gates they saw two guards working the keypad and opening the gates. They waved them in and Anna waved back to them as they started up the long drive. The others looked out the windows and watched the front yard of the King of Rock n'

Roll go by.  She pulled up to the back of the house and made sure they were under the covered car port at the back.  They entered through the kitchen.

"You know, we could actually cook ourselves a real meal tonight," said Ismaele opening the refrigerator.  "They have the whole place stocked."

"I leave the meal preparation in your very capable hands," said Anna.

"I could use some assistance."

"I'll help," said Verdi.

"Alright, let's look through this thing and see what we can find."  Zaccaria, Abadallo and Anna decided to look for entertainment elsewhere.  The place had been changed very little from its time as a museum.  They walked into the jungle room and saw the TVs.  The only difference being people had hooked up some old school video games to them.  Zaccaria and Abadallo sat down and grabbed the controllers to the last Nintendo in existence.  They started up Super Mario Bros. while Anna lounged in the big chair.  They played and bickered like they had as children.  Anna laughed and played when Zaccaria got tired of it and was pouting because Abadallo hadn't let him get the fire flower.

"Ever play this Anna?" Zaccaria asked as he was surprised at her ease with the whole game.

"I was an only child with five boys for friends," said Anna with a smirk.  "They were in the neighboring houses on either side of us.  Of course I played this.  I got to play all of these games with them."

"And I'm guessing you bested them at all of these games!"  Anna jumped over a particularly prickly enemy with ease while Zaccaria fell into the pit.

"Oh yeah, I was the coolest girl on the block."

"How do you figure?"

"If the other boys picked on my friends, I would help them win at the games."  Zaccaria laughed and shook his head.  Soon they started to smell something wonderful drifting into the room.

"What all did Ismaele find in that kitchen?" asked Abadallo.

"I have no idea," said Anna. "My suggestion is if it looks weird but smells good, shut up and eat it. You don't want to know what it is and you don't want to know what he did to make it taste like that."

In the kitchen things were going very well. They had cooked some meat with some vegetables and were putting together a spaghetti sauce with the canned tomatoes. Ismaele also decided to make some biscuits to go along with the meal.

"We should make a desert," said Verdi in agreement to Ismaele's thought. Ismaele smiled and straightened up.

"What do you think we should make?" he asked taking off his oven mitts.

"Something easy," said Verdi. Ismaele nodded in agreement. He started peeling a few apples on the counter and humming quietly to himself.

"What is that you're humming?" asked Verdi.

"I have no idea. My mother used to hum it while she was cooking. It helps me to concentrate when I'm trying to remember a recipe that she taught me."

"You have recipes memorized."

"All the ones my mother taught me. She didn't like cookbooks. She wrote down recipes once so if she forgot a step or an ingredient she could refer back. But otherwise she did everything from memory and sight. Sometimes she could tell if a dish just wasn't right just by the look of it. She didn't even have to taste it." He continued humming as he peeled the apples. Verdi started making another batch of biscuit dough while Ismaele tossed the apples into a bowl. He added sugar, cinnamon and a little bit of lemon juice and tossed them all together. Verdi was cutting the dough into circles and Ismaele wrapped each slice of apple in a biscuit. He knew there was vanilla ice cream in the freezer and they could serve them with ice cream. It would be a nice end to a nice meal. They put their creation on a cookie sheet and got everything else ready to be served. Verdi walked into the jungle room and found an interesting sight to say the least. Anna was sitting on Zaccaria's back while she and Abadallo went head to head on a Sonic game.

142

"Why are you sitting on him?" he asked with some trepidation.

"He lost," said Anna and Abadallo together. Verdi shrugged figuring it was as good an explanation as any.

"Dinner's almost ready. Time to come to the table."

"Two minutes," said Abadallo. They were nearing the end of the course and suddenly Anna cut ahead and claimed the lead. "How did you-?"

"Don't stop to wonder, run!" shouted Verdi. Abadallo continued on but Anna's lead cinched it. She had won the race.

"Ha HA!" she said jumping to her feet. Zaccaria got up with a groan. "I get to sit on you for the next game!" she said pointing at Abadallo.

"Best two out of three!" Abadallo whined.

"Dinner time!" said Verdi with more authority than they had ever heard before. It shocked them so much that they immediately fell silent and went out the door. They assembled at the dinner table and quietly waited for Ismaele to join them. The cornbread and spinach madeleine were already sitting on the table. Now he appeared with the perfectly seasoned pork loin on a plate. They couldn't stop from staring at all this magnificent food hungrily. Ismaele put the plate down and said,

"Anyone want to say grace?" They nervously looked at each other until Verdi said,

"I'll do it." They bowed their heads and closed their eyes. "Thank you for this food, thank you for this place to stay. Thank you for friends, protectors and soldiers. Thank you for the opportunity to change things in this crazy world. Please let this mission not been in vain. Please let my words and my actions make a difference and be worthy of the actions of these fine people with me now. Amen."

"Amen," they chorused quietly. They all sat down and began serving each other. First part of dinner was as usual in any household. Various requests for dishes and condiments and extra butter. They felt odd. This was the nicest house any of them had been in for three years now. And it wasn't their house. It wasn't even a house the last time any of them had been in it. It was a

143

museum.  Now it was a house again.  The best hiding place in a world gone mad and no one was sure why it was so protected.  Maybe just because music was such a universal thing.  Elvis never meant anyone any harm.  He only wanted to make music and bring joy to the world.  There were only a few other places like this.  They were all places that used to be centers of music.  Homes and studios and museums and halls.  They were all still places considered sacred by everyone left behind.

Anna dug into her food and found it delicious immediately.  She smiled at Ismaele.

"This is a really good meal you and Verdi have cooked for us here Izzy," she said with a smile.

"Thank you very much Anna," said Ismaele returning the smile.  "Your name is too short to shorten this time around."

"I know," said Anna sipping on a beer.  "Just as well.  That last name was atrocious."

"What was your name last time?" asked Verdi.

"Hortense."  Verdi nearly choked on his cornbread when he heard the name.  Zaccaria was laughing but still leaned over and gave Verdi a couple of careful whacks to the back.

"Easy there tiger," said Zaccaria.  "That was it.  That was her name."

"Should have known it would end badly when I got a name like that."

"What did…?  I hate to ask this but what did the others shorten it to?"

"It's not what you're thinking," she said with a shake of her head.  Verdi raised an eyebrow.

"Ok, what then?"

"Ory."

"Ory?"

"Ory."

"She's right," said Abadallo.  "We knew she would beat us up if we called her… well, the name you're thinking of.  The compromise became Ory."

"I still hated it," said Anna.

"But, she didn't hit us," said Ismaele. "Wasn't like the rest of us got real stellar names on that trip." Verdi put down his knife and fork.

"Wait; let me swallow before you continue." The others waited patiently until Verdi did swallow. "Alright, hit me."

"Well, I was Percy," said Ismaele. "It got shortened to P because I couldn't take being called "Perce"."

"I was Commodus," said Zaccaria.

"Wait, like the emperor…?"

"Who was in love with his sister and all? Yep, same one."

"What did that get shortened to? Or do I even want to know?"

"Odus." Verdi started laughing as did the others.

"Odus?"

"Commy just sounded weird. Comm was too much like our shortening for referring to our communications system. And well… Odus just stuck one day."

"And you?" Verdi was looking at Abadallo who was staring at his plate. He really hoped he wouldn't have to bring up the name he had been given.

"Go ahead, tell him," said Zaccaria.

"Dick," said Abadallo. There was a pause. And then laughter came sputtering out of Verdi like an outboard motor. The others began to laugh as well.

"What… what did… it didn't get any shorter did it?" said Verdi trying to breathe.

"Wouldn't have made it any better or worse," said Abadallo stabbing at his food.

"It is funny Dallo," said Zaccaria.

"Yours was funnier, Zac," said Abadallo sticking out his tongue.

"Well, you all seem to have adapted to your current names," said Verdi looking at them.

"These have been far easier to live with than many of the others," said Anna.

"Why don't you like yours then?" asked Verdi. She glared at him hard and he looked down at his plate. "Sorry, hazard of conversation. I hear thoughts better when people are talking to me."

"It was my daughter's name," Anna said softly. Everyone around the table stopped. "I haven't spoken it in three years. I haven't even said my own name in three years. It's almost like treading on some kind of holy ground. I keep waiting for some priest to come and scold me for saying the wrong thing." She swallowed hard and sipped on her beer. "Anyway, let's just keep eating." They turned back to their plates and continued to eat. Anna tried to maintain. After a few minutes she got up from the table with her beer and went out into the back yard. Verdi started to stand but Ismaele said,

"No, leave her be for now. Later. She'll be more receptive later. I can promise you that." Verdi sat down and yielded to Ismaele's better judgment. They continued to eat, but the mood had become subdued. After a while, Zaccaria and Abadallo gathered the plates and put away the leftovers in the fridge. Ismaele retreated to the jungle room to brush up on his gaming skills before the others came in. Verdi went into the back yard to find Anna.

She was sitting in front of Elvis's grave. She had lit a candle and was staring into the flame.

"There used to be an eternal flame here," she said as Verdi walked up. "I guess the fuel stopped being replenished so it went out. Nothing is eternal, I suppose." Verdi walked over to her and put a gentle hand on her shoulder.

"I'm sorry," he said quietly. "I really am. I'm sorry. I didn't know-"

"Of course you didn't know. Even the men I travel with didn't know my daughter's name until tonight. If they did, they would have been just as shocked as I was when I was given this code name. Like the opera or something?"

"It's one of my favorites. I was in a production of it once." Anna looked up at him in surprise. But in truth when she thought about it, it wasn't really all that surprising.

"Who were you?"

"Ismaele. I loved my part. I loved the music. I loved everything about it."

"Kind of surprising that you could perform."

"I know. It's hard to explain. Being in the music world, one can be a prima donna who rarely has an audience with anyone personally and insists on being left alone before every show. I got to know the people I was with. I often played with the same people over and over. I don't know if they knew. Who knows what all of us knew. In a world like that you are allowed to be odd."

"Tell me about it." Anna finished her beer and stared into the flame of the candle.

"You were a musician? Back in the old days?" She laughed a bitter sarcastic laugh.

"Yeah, back a long time ago when the earth was still habitable I was a musician. I danced on waves of music and light and believed that anything was possible as long as I tried hard enough."

"What did you play?"

"No... I'll tell you that later. When we're closer to New York." Verdi looked at her confused. "You keep secrets, I'll keep secrets."

"Hardly a-"

"Comparison? I don't really care. You have a secret. You think you have a way out of this. I don't care if it works or it doesn't. I don't really care what it is. Yet I still want to know. It won't change anything. I'll still protect you all the way to New York and make sure that you do whatever it is that you want to do. Knowing what instrument I played isn't going to change anything. But I'm keeping that to myself. I'll tell you when we're closer to New York."

"Where are we stopping before we get there?"

"Washington D.C. Might even sleep in the White House."

"THE White House?"

"There is only one White House in the whole town."

"I didn't think it was still standing."

147

"It's still there. And it's the one building that has the most lead shielding in the whole town. While we're there, I'll tell you what instrument I played. And then you'll tell me what your grand plan is." She slowly stood on wobbly legs and he reached out and grabbed her arm. They looked at each other and for a moment, Verdi felt all the blinding emotional pain she was in at that moment. The feel of it almost made the earth give out from under his feet. She saw that the contact was doing to him and quickly pulled away.

"Don't, just don't, you don't want to go there," she said to him.

"Anna, I-"

"What? Is it so weird that I don't want you in my mind that easily?"

"I understand that, more than you realize."

"I doubt that."

"No, no I do. I do understand that. But I could help you."

"You can help? How can you help? What can you do?"

"I- I can't explain how I can help all I can tell you is that I can!"

"Some kind of Jedi mind trick? Make me think everything is just sunshine and light and rainbows."

"I'm not that good."

"Then how good are you?" Verdi did his next move quickly so that she wouldn't stop him. He rushed forward and laid a hand on each of her cheeks. And for a few seconds, he took her pain from her. He eased her mind for a few moments and let her believe that things would be alright and there was a purpose. He felt his heart beat hard and strain under the weight but he didn't let go. She reached out and rubbed a thumb over his furrowed brow. His expression eased and his hands moved to her shoulders as he let go of the pain in her mind. She felt the same, yet better. She looked at him with some uncertainty as to what had happened.

"What did...?"

"I don't know," he said quietly. "Feel better though?" She shuffled and thought for a second.

"Yeah… I kinda do.  Are you okay?"

"I do that rarely.  It's draining.  Good night's sleep is all I need right now."  She walked him back into the house and they chose one of the bedrooms for him at the far end of the house. She went back into the jungle room to found the boys playing Mario Bros. ecstatically.  They paused for a second when she walked in.

"Where's Verdi?" asked Ismaele.

"I put him to bed," she said taking off her coat.  "You boys look like you could use some competition."  For the next three hours, they took turns going at the game.  They beat each other's high scores, they trounced each other's enemies and they played several games late into the night.  Zaccaria and Abadallo fell asleep together in the corner.  Ismaele and Anna were still playing late that night.  She beat him for the third time in a row and he finally threw down the controller.

"I'm beat," he said looking at his watch.  "And no wonder I'm beat, it's 2 am."

"It's been a very long time since I've stayed up late playing games," she said turning off the game system so that she wouldn't be tempted into playing more by herself.  "When should we roll out?"

"Where's our next stop?"

"Washington D. C.  15 hour drive."  Ismaele sneered and shuddered.

"How much farther after that?"

"Five hours, depending on where he wants to go in New York City."

"Does anyone know where we're going exactly?"

"I don't know if anyone ever asked.  Just the mention of New York City is enough to make people sit up and take notice."

"We should ask him tomorrow."

"Right, one of the many things we'll find out tomorrow."

"Many things?"

"I'm hoping to discover the origin of the universe, learn to restring a guitar and know what his master plan is by the end of the day."

149

"Busy day. We should start at 8 am."

"Sounds like a plan to me." Anna leaned over and shook Zaccaria awake.

"Zac, you two should get to a real bed," she said to his sleepy face. He nodded and nudged Abadallo into wakefulness. The two shuffled off to a bed they had marked for themselves. Anna and Ismaele also went to separate beds. All were so tired they were asleep by the time their heads hit the pillows.

Meanwhile...

"They've reached Memphis," said the dark haired man. "There shouldn't be much resistance." The red head stared at the point on the map that they were heading for.

"There were only four with him," she replied.

"That shouldn't be a problem." The radio crackled.

"There's an army here!" shouted a voice through the radio. They both looked at the radio and then at each other. The sounds of battle and screams and explosions bled through until the radio went dead.

"Only four?"

"There's only four with him! There must have been others taking refuge in Memphis."

"And why didn't you warn us about that?"

"I can't feel what's ahead of him! Just where he is. And when I checked he was only with four people. That's the only way he would be comfortable."

"Doesn't matter. We'll catch up with them soon. And then he won't be a problem anymore."

# Chapter 10

Sometime around 6 am Anna was woken by a noise. She couldn't tell what the noise was or where it was coming from, but she knew it wasn't right. She got out of bed and got her gun. She could tell it was somewhere in the house. Ismaele met her in the hallway. He also had his gun drawn. They shuffled down the hallway looking for the source of the sound. Zaccaria and Abadallo both emerged from their room fully dressed, also looking curious. They slowly walked through the house until they got to the room where Verdi had been sleeping all night. They could hear the weird noise through the door. Anna slowly opened the door and surveyed the room. They couldn't see Verdi anywhere. But there was blood on the walls and two dead raiders lying on the floor. Anna looked to the others and then back down at them. She looked outside the window and saw guards lying dead on the ground. There were only two questions on their mind. Where was Verdi? And why were they still alive and had never been awakened by the raiders? Their bodies were cool. This had happened a little while after going to bed. Anna listened carefully and realized the weird sound was coming from the closet. She slowly opened it and found Verdi sitting on the floor of the closet, rocking back and forth and humming to himself. He was covered in blood and still holding a knife. Anna approached first.

"Verdi?" she whispered gently. "Verdi?" She was hesitant but she touched him lightly on the shoulder. She jumped back when he swung the knife. She raised her arms and said to him calmly, "It's okay, Verdi. It's just me." The others were still pointing their guns and Verdi started to swing again. This time Anna caught his arm and pinned it to her side. She pulled the knife from his hand and threw it into the wall. "It's me, Verdi. It's Anna." She took his hand and gently put it to the side of her head.

He looked at her like someone trying to remember someone from years ago or someone trying very hard to come out of a daze.

"Anna?" he whispered. His fingers lightly stroked her cheek and she held his hand there.

"Yes, Verdi. It's me Anna. What happened here?" Verdi looked down and saw the bodies. He started to retreat back into the closet but she grabbed hold of his arms and wouldn't let him. "Oh no you don't, let's get you out of this room if you're going to react to them like that." She and Ismaele pulled Verdi from the room while Zaccaria and Abadallo stepped outside to take a look around. They walked down the street towards Sun Studio. It was as they had feared. The lure of Verdi, it seemed, had made even the most sacred of holy grounds fair game. People were lying dead. Shot, stabbed and in a few cases beaten to death. But that wasn't the weirdest part of this whole scene. There was no one else. There was no one left. Many of the people they knew were dead but so were many of the raiders. The place had taken on an eerie quiet that they couldn't shake.

Meanwhile, Ismaele and Anna were getting Verdi cleaned up and dressed. He only had a few bruises and scratches. Nothing matched the blood loss they found him covered in. He had stopped humming, but he wasn't talking either. Something had happened in that room that they really needed to know. Anna was shocked that he had so few wounds on him. The raiders in his room had been armed to the teeth with every kind of weapon. But they never got to use those weapons it seemed. Otherwise, Verdi would have been a dead man. She sat down in front of him and held his hands gently.

"Verdi, I know it's hard and I'm really not sure what it is that you went through in the very early morning hours. But whatever happened, we've all done our share of crazy and bad things. There will be no judgment; I can assure you of that." Verdi stared down at her hands and didn't answer for a few minutes. Finally he took just her right hand into his two.

"The raiders came two hours ago," he whispered. "Everyone at Sun Studio woke up and took them on. Some of the raiders ran when they saw many people here. Some of the people at Sun Studios ran. The ones who had no means or ability to fight. Only two of the raiders broke away from them and headed here. They were running down the street. Trying to get here. Trying to get me. They were trying to tempt me. They killed the few guards who hadn't run to defend Sun Studios. They wanted me to come out and give myself up. They wanted my secrets. I wouldn't. It didn't make them happy. They came in. I... I..." Ismaele and Anna looked at each other. They could guess what happened next from the scene they found in the room. "I've only ever been in the presence of someone dying twice before. It felt like sinking and dying. I've never killed anyone before. They wanted to... they wanted to kill you all. They wanted to do terrible... terrible things. I couldn't let that happen. I just... I don't know how I did it I just..."

"It's okay, Verdi, you don't have to tell us," said Anna. Verdi looked up at her. His eyes were unreadable. It worried her.

"I felt them dying. They were dying because of what I did. God what I did..."

"It's alright," said Ismaele. "Out of everyone in the world we understand."

"I couldn't let them... I couldn't let them stop this... I couldn't let them know what I know... All the things that I know..." He started to rock back and forth again and started mumbling to himself all the same things over and over again. He let go of Anna's hand and put his hands over his ears. Anna made a bid for his sanity and took his face in her hands like he had done to her the night before.

"Verdi," she said calmly but with some authority. He stopped rocking and looked at her. "I know. I know how much it hurts to kill someone. Being who you are, I can't imagine how much it must hurt right now. What we're trying to tell you is we do not fear you. We do not blame you. And we're not disgusted with you. We understand. You don't have to explain yourself and you don't have to tell us what you did to keep us and yourself safe. We can guess. It's okay."

"I didn't know I could... that I could do that."

155

"No one ever does. Not until they are in the situation."
Abadallo and Zaccaria walked back into the room. Anna and
Ismaele could tell by their faces what they had found outside.

"We need to get moving soon," said Ismaele. Anna
nodded.

"Verdi, we need to get you in the car. Okay?" Verdi
nodded mutely. He reached for his iPod and blindfold. Anna
helped him to shut out the world around him and then put him in
the car. The others packed and loaded the car. Anna took the
wheel for the first of their trip. They rode silently through the city
seeing the bodies of their friends scattered about. They pieced
together the scene as they rolled through the city. Their friends
had outnumbered the raiders ten to one. But the raiders had
automatic weapons and flame throwers. Sun Studio was in ruin.
The raider's vehicles were burned up. The raiders who had
stayed and fought were dead. Their friends had fought gloriously.
But now the city wasn't safe and they had abandoned the place.
Anna turned onto the interstate and they put Memphis behind
them.

## Meanwhile

"We're closing in on them fast," said the dark-haired man. "They've been driving all day but we're still gaining on them."

"It's been a lot easier to track them since he's slept most of the day," said the red head from her reclining position on the back seat.

"I suppose if he knew we were onto him he wouldn't sleep nearly as much. Are you looking forward to seeing him again." The red head chuckled slowly.

"Oh brother mine... I... seeee... you..."

# Chapter 11

They had to be careful. They knew that raiders were gathering. Ismaele got on the radio to Snake and checked to see that things were the same. They also were able to send out a message to everyone that Memphis was now unsafe. Anna drove until lunch time. They didn't feel safe getting out of the car even in broad daylight. So they opened cans of fruit and soup and ate in the car. Verdi came out of his world of music and dark for lunch. There wasn't much conversation. Snake had confirmed that their path was still safe. Abadallo took over the wheel since there were still several hours of daylight. Anna crawled into the back seat next to Verdi. Verdi had already retreated into his dark world and she didn't have the heart to try to break him out of it. She dozed for a bit and started to wake up when she started falling to the side. Arms caught her and eased her down. She went back to sleep quickly and didn't think about where she was or who had caught her. After all, everyone in the car she trusted.

Ismaele was watching the horizon in the passenger seat and Zaccaria had retreated to the back to watch for raiders. Verdi had sensed rather than saw her start to fall to the seat. He reached out in reaction and let her settle back to sleep on his leg. He took off his blindfold and took out his ear buds and looked down at her. In sleep she was very peaceful looking. Almost child-like even. She started to twitch and he knew she was in the middle of a nightmare. He didn't usually touch people without their knowing. He always felt it a breach of confidence. Especially when they were sleeping. People's brains were always so much more unguarded when they were sleeping. All the terrors and monsters and secrets they kept on lock-down during the day would come busting out of their bonds and dance around the room. He knew if he did nothing she would be waking up soon and shouting at all of them.  He touched the back of her neck and whispered to her quietly,

"It's alright.  Everything's alright."

~

He saw what she saw.  Bodies strewn on the ground.  Cut to pieces and staring up at her with lifeless eyes.  She was tied down and being cut up.  He had gleaned bits from their conversation.  He knew the last mission they went on was this.  A save the world mission that nearly killed her.  He could feel the knife cutting into her skin and nearly screamed in pain along with her.  She was helpless.  She couldn't fight.  Her companions in this version of events were dead already.  Cut to pieces on the floor and staring up helplessly.  Verdi decided to do something he knew was dangerous.  He might lose her trust forever.  But he couldn't let this nightmare continue.  Still in the dream, he imagined himself at the entrance to the cave.

"Stop now or I will shoot!" he shouted.  He was surprised at how big of a gun he had chosen for this.  But it was a dream after all.  She looked at him.  She was surprised.  She was shocked.

"Verdi?" she whispered.  With a sneer the madman lowered his knife to her flesh again.  Verdi fired without hesitation.  This was a dream after all.  Killing a figment of someone's imagination bothered him less than squashing a bug.  The madman was spattered across the back wall.  He dropped his weapon and walked to the bodies on the floor.  "What are you...?"

"Remember, remember what actually happened here," he said calmly.  The bodies of her four companions knit themselves back together under his hands.  "This wasn't how things played out."  The companions stood and charged the bamboo cage they were now trapped in.  The madman was back, but only for a moment as Zaccaria launched himself over her and took the man's head with one stroke of his knife.  The others went to her and pulled her from the stone altar.  Verdi saw a second vision of her dressed and standing against the wall.  He walked to her and they watched as the scene played out the way it had happened.  They washed her wounds.  Bandaged and shivering, Ismaele took off his shirt and held her naked body to his chest to keep her warm.  Abadallo swaddled the rest of her in a blanket to keep her warm and then they ran out of the cave.

"I don't... remember any of that..." whispered the version of her next to him.  Verdi took her hand and squeezed it tight.

"I know.  But they do.  It hasn't left their mind since this mission started.  Just like it hasn't left yours.  But you need to remember, they saved you once when the odds were stacked and the chances were slim.  They would do it again in a heartbeat."

They weren't in the cave anymore.  They were in the hospital and she was shivering on the bed.

"I don't remember anything of these three days," she said quietly.  Her companions walked in and saw her.  Ismaele moved her gently and got into bed with her.  She watched as in sleep she moved towards him and settled on his chest.  The doctor started to protest but Abadallo put his protests down.  They watched as she calmed.  She got better.  And three days later, she was walking out of the room with Ismaele at her side.

"He didn't leave you," said Verdi.  "None of them did."

"I've had nightmares about this... these six days, for a year now.  Every single night, for a whole damn year."

"It's time you slept peacefully for once.  Think of something happy.  Somewhere you would love to be right now."  The scene changed around them.  Bright sunlight through trees, green grass grew beneath their feet, a calm breeze through their hair and she heard a giggle she hadn't heard in three years.  Holding her breath, she turned around slowly.  She saw what she expected.

Herself, her husband and her daughter on that last picnic together.  Her daughter was gathering flowers and throwing them onto Anna's face.  Anna and her husband were both laughing.

"I can't..." she muttered shaking her head.

"Yes, you can," said Verdi gently.  "Here you can.  All you have to do is step forward and live through this memory.  That's all.  You can stay as long as you like."  She walked forward slowly until she was even with her own feet.  She lay down in the same spot and opened her eyes as her husband leaned down to kiss her.  Verdi watched.  She didn't hesitate.  She responded to the kiss in kind and then laughed again when their daughter threw flowers at them saying,

"No yucky stuff!!"

~

Verdi took his hand off her neck and left the dream world she was in. She wasn't fidgeting anymore. She slept peacefully. He looked around for a second but no one was looking at them. They had assumed both were asleep. Verdi put back in his headphones and put back on his blindfold and enclosed himself. He was losing energy. He had to conserve all the energy he could.

Anna slept for the next eight hours. No one thought to wake her. No one wanted to since it was the first time any of them had seen her do that in a year. They finally woke her and Verdi when they stopped for dinner. Ismaele was waiting for the swing that she usually woke up with, but her eyes slowly opened and she turned to him slowly.

"You sleep okay?" Ismaele asked gently.

"Yeah, best sleep in a year," she said stretching. "Why?"

"You've been asleep for eight hours." She frowned and looked about. She realized where she was and straightened up with an apologetic look.

"Sorry," she started to mutter.

"Don't be," said Ismaele gently. "It was good to see you sleep for a change." Verdi took off his blindfold and ear buds and folded them up like he always did.

"Sorry I slept on you," she said to him.

"Don't be," he said with a pat on her shoulder. "I could have moved you if I wanted to." Maybe she thought it was just a dream. Maybe she didn't realize that he had actually been in her mind. Didn't matter. He wasn't about to end the illusion. Zaccaria poured through the bag of provisions and passed some out. Anna was counting up the hours and miles.

"How much longer until we reach Washington?" she asked.

"About another three, maybe four hours," said Abadallo. "Zac probably needs to drive from here on. It's gotten dark."

162

Anna looked out the windows and tried to remember how she managed to sleep so well.

"I'll sit at the back then," said Ismaele. "Abadallo, you should get some sleep. Anna, you up for keeping Zac company?"

"Sure," she said drinking the last of the syrup from the peach can. They shifted to their given positions and the car started again. It would be only a few hours until they were at their next to last destination. A crackle came over the radio. Zaccaria and Anna looked back as Ismaele picked up the receiver.

"Blackbird here," he said quietly into the receiver. There was static. More static. Then a small whisper over the radio that made Verdi sit up straight trembling said,

"I... seee.... you...." Verdi ripped off his blindfold and ear buds.

"Drive!! Drive now and drive fast!!" he shouted at Zaccaria.

"What's wrong?" said Anna. An explosion to their right nearly knocked the car over. Zaccaria didn't wait for an answer and put the gas pedal down.

"My God I've put you all in danger," Verdi whispered. "She followed me. She followed me here!" Anna climbed into the back and grabbed him by the shoulders.

"Who? Who followed you?"

"She... she..."

"Who is she Verdi?!" Another explosion broke the window and she shielded his face with her jacket.

"I SEE YOU!" said the voice over the radio again. Verdi screamed and held his head. He felt like his brain was boiling inside his skull. He could just barely feel Anna trying to shake him out of it. He knew she was yelling but he couldn't hear her anymore. All he could hear was the constant screaming in his head.

Anna couldn't figure out what had happened. She stood on the seat and peered out the sun roof. There was one Humvee following them. One of their men was on the rocket launcher. She aimed well with her gun and took him out. But he was dumped on the side of the road and another took his place. She felt a hand tugging her down and she dropped to her knees on the seat. She turned and was face to face with Verdi.

"It's been her," he said through gritted teeth. She could see the physical toll this was taking on him to talk to her through the pain he was in. "It's been her the whole time."

"Who is she?" said Anna trying to keep Verdi with them.

"My twin sister. Yes, she's a telepath just like me. That's how she's been tracking us."

"Evil twin I'm guessing?"

"You could put it that way." He took several deep breaths and squeezed her hand tighter. "Stop the car."

"Zac, pull over."

"Are you crazy?" said Zaccaria looking in the rearview mirror at them.

"Just pull over," said Verdi. Something in his voice made Zaccaria pull them over to the side of the road.

"They're pulling over too," said Ismaele. Verdi took several deep breaths and looked to Anna. Anna nodded and opened the door. All of them stepped out of the vehicle and into the middle of the street. Verdi stood in front of them. Across the street, the door to the other Humvee opened. Out stepped a woman who was Verdi's almost mirror opposite. Her hair was bright red, her eyes black as coal and her skin pasty white. Three men got out and stood behind her as well. The two telepaths approached each other. Anna followed Verdi and one man followed his sister. The others turned away and watched the road from each direction.

"Andrew," said the woman in greeting.

"Adriana," he replied.

"What name are you going by now?"

"Verdi."

"God, that stupid opera fixation of yours."

"And you?"

"Beatrice Quinn." Anna almost felt her heart jump in her throat. Especially since she said Beatrice the Italian way so it sounded so pretty: Bea-tree-che.

"I get the comic books reference... but, Shakespeare?"

"Hawthorne." Verdi rolled his eyes in disgust.

"The girl who couldn't be touched? Is that what you're trying to say sis? If a man gets close to you they will die?"

"You should know better than anyone."

"I do know you better than anyone and that's not who you are sis."

"Better the side in power than the side cowering in fear."

"Not cowering. Just on a mission."

"About that."

"What?"

"Don't."

"Don't what?"

"Don't do it. Don't go on this mission."

"I don't even know if this will work sis!"

"But you've given the people hope Verdi. Hope for a future better than this one."

"Is that what your man is afraid of Quinn? Hope?" Quinn shifted uneasily and glanced back for a second with only her eyes. "Yes, I know you're not the mastermind behind all of this. Just the bloodhound."

"Oh but she is such a very good bitch," said a voice from the open door of the car. A man with bronzed skin, shoulder-length dark hair and equally dark eyes stepped out of the vehicle and looked straight at Verdi.

"And you are?"

"Gray. I've been tracking you for the last few days trying to stop your mission. Your sister has been most helpful. But you know that, don't you?"

"I never used her like you do."

"I can't really understand why."

"Why are you so dead set on stopping me?"

"You heard her. You've given the people hope. Hope. It's a very dangerous thing. Almost as dangerous as a real name. Like the real name of your friend behind you." Verdi fell to his knees screaming at that moment. Anna raised her gun and pointed it at Quinn.

165

"You stop that right now or I will blow your head off!" she shouted with authority in her voice.

"She doesn't listen to you," said Gray with a sneer.

"She'll listen to a bullet!"

"She is capable of multi-tasking you know. The men behind you could be like him very easily. Only they can't take the mental beating he can." Anna hesitated.

"He's in agony!"

"Then give me your name! End his reason to fight!" Anna looked down at Verdi crumpled on the ground. Every instinct in her body screamed to not tell. But she needed this man to live. He had given hope to the people. His plan might actually work.

"Beatrice Anna DeRousseau!" Verdi was still screaming at her feet. "That's my real name! Now let him go!" Gray ran her name through a tracker and nodded to Quinn. Verdi stopped screaming and reached out for Anna's boot. Anna kneeled down and pulled the still crumpled man into her lap.

"It's going to be okay," she muttered to him quietly. "Don't worry; it's going to be okay."

"I can't take much more of this," he whispered to her desperately.

"You were a cello player," said Gray looking at her profile. "Your last known location was New York. You had a husband and a child who are still in New York. They're dead aren't they?"

"Been dead three years now," she said in a matter-of-fact tone.

"And now you're going back to the city you abandoned. Why?"

"He said that's where he needs to go." Gray walked over to her. She remained kneeling on the ground next to Verdi.

"And you're just a good little soldier taking this mad man wherever he needs to go."

"He said he has a way to fix things. And I hate what this world has become. I've followed 33 other mad men into their crazy plans to save this world. He's the first who actually believed what he was going to do might not work. It may sound crazy to

166

you but that actually made us all feel better. We thought what he had in mind might at least be worth the time."

"You still don't know what his plan is, do you?" Gray slowly kneeled down on the other side of Verdi. She felt Verdi's arms come around her waist tightly. Something Gray was thinking terrified him.

"I don't." She reached down and put a hand on his head soothingly. "I don't really care. Why do you care so much about one man on a crazy mission to fix this world?"

"You see dear, I am a business man. I deal in fear. As long as I can keep everyone afraid, keep them suspicious of everyone who comes by, as long as I can keep them believing that the only way to keep themselves safe is to pay me in food, fuel, jewels, women, my life and the lives of my men, go on. You get a madman like this one; people start to hope that their lives just might be better. That maybe they could trust those wandering players. That maybe they could form alliances with others. And even, possibly, join forces and fight people like me. That's just... unacceptable." Verdi was quick. He pulled the knife from Anna's belt and stabbed Gray in the chest. Anna wasn't sure who was more surprised, her or Gray who was now staring at the two of them with wide eyes. She felt more than saw Verdi's entire body tense as the light of life went out in the Gray's eyes. She reached forward and pulled the knife out of the man's chest. In doing so, she pulled Verdi away from the man and back towards her. She quickly stood and pulled Verdi up with her. She could see the murderous intent on the faces of the men and she aimed her gun with her free arm.

"Don't!" she shouted at them. "Just don't! We're heading out to see if this crazy plan of his works. If you want to continue this conversation, meet us in New York in two days." The men looked to Quinn. She nodded and the new leader had been decided. Anna put one of Verdi's arms around her shoulders and walked him back to the Humvee.

"What do we do now?" asked Ismaele.

"Just get in the damn car and let's get to Washington." Verdi was breaking apart. She could feel it without him even saying a word. She pushed him into his old spot in the car and sat down next to him.

"Stay with me Verdi," she whispered to him. Zaccaria got into the driver's seat, Abadallo in the passenger seat and Ismael opened the back window and watched the raiders and the town they had been in disappear behind them. They were silent. All except Verdi and Anna.

## Meanwhile...

The red head got back into the Humvee and watched the opposing vehicle drive away with her brother in it.

"Why did you let them go?" asked the driver.

"The Boss was good, but he didn't know my brother," she replied. "He'll either lose his nerve before he gets there, the others will kill him once they know his plan or he'll find some other way to get killed. That's the way he is."

"And if he does make it to New York?"

"Then we'll kill him there." The Humvee sped away in a dust cloud.

"Should we pursue them?"

"No. We'll get ahead of them and meet them in New York. We can use the paths through Virginia that they will be too scared to take. Let's go." The driver took a sharp turn and headed for the northern highways that were controlled by the raiders.

# Chapter 12

Verdi was screaming. The three men in the car felt completely helpless. They knew that between his sister's attacks on his mind and killing another person he had to be in intense mental pain and anguish. But there was nothing they could do. Anna was desperately trying to break through to him like she'd done before and bring him back down to reality. But it seemed like every time she touched him he would scream louder. She realized after a couple of tries that his brain was over-sensitized. Her touch kept transferring all she was feeling and it was close to killing him. She suddenly had a plan. She pulled his long sleeves down. She grabbed his iPod and searched for a specific piece. She checked the volume on herself before putting the ear buds in his ears. From the level of his screaming he couldn't hear it through the screaming in his brain. She tied his blindfold around his eyes and then she put his hand to the back of her neck. The piece she had chosen was one of the Bach cello suites that she had played so often she knew it by heart.

"What are you doing?" asked Ismaele.

"Just don't disturb us for a while," she said calmly. "I'm not as stupid as people like to think I am, Verdi." Her hand covered his on the back of her neck and she imagined herself playing the cello suite he was listening to.

~

Suddenly, she was in a concert hall. She was playing her old cello. She was still wearing her black clothes and boots. She looked around and saw that it was her favorite room at Carnegie Hall. The Weill Recital Hall. There was shouting and screaming outside the doors. But Verdi was sitting in the front row. His elbows on his knees, arms crossed and his head resting on his arms. Bruised and battered and bleeding, he was dressed in rags and trying to catch his breath. She continued to play the cello suite she had put on for him to listen to. It was one of her favorites out of the set. She didn't speak as Verdi slowly looked up at her. He looked back at the doors at the back. The shouting and screaming could still be heard, but he saw heavy chains and padlocks on the doors keeping those things out. They couldn't even turn the door handles because the chains were so heavy.

"Anna?" he whispered as if talking too loud would break this dream. She smiled at him gently with a nod of her head and continued to play. "Anna, what's going on?" She didn't acknowledge the question and continued to play. He walked forward and grabbed at her foot. "Anna!" She stopped playing now and looked at him incredulously.

"Is that how you act at a concert?" she asked him calmly. He stopped and looked down at himself. He was wearing a tuxedo. He looked up at her and she was now wearing a bright red dress with matching shoes. Her dark hair hung down in loose curls around her neck and her face was perfectly done with makeup and lipstick. He turned and saw a whole crowd of people in their finery sitting in the seats behind him. They were all looking at him with gentle confusion. The shouting outside had stopped. "I'll have to start all over again." He turned back to her and bowed nervously.

"I'm sorry. I didn't realize where I was."

"Now that you know where you are, will you please take your seat?" He turned back to see a beautiful redhead in the front row patting the seat next to her. "Just an observation, but I think she likes you." He smiled half in disbelief and half in relief and sat down in the seat that the gorgeous woman had saved for him. She easily slid her hand into his and smiled at him warmly.

"I apologize for my friend ladies and gentlemen," said Anna smoothly. "I will start again." She started playing again and everyone was enthralled by her playing. Verdi felt himself smile the first genuine smile he had smiled in a long time. Here, in this moment, he was happy.

~

Verdi had stopped screaming. He was quiet. Completely quiet. Anna still sat with his hand on the back of her neck. The others weren't sure what was happening and didn't quite know what to do. But he was quiet again. And they still had a few hours' drive to make. Whatever she had done to get him quiet, they didn't want to ruin it.

By the time they got through the checkpoints around Washington and pulled up to the White House, Verdi was asleep in Anna's lap. Anna was sitting up but slumped over in sleep as well. The rest of the trip had been uneventful. Once parked and ready to go in the building, Zaccaria shook Anna awake. She woke slowly and looked up.

"We've made it to Washington," said Zaccaria. She nodded and gently prodded Verdi awake. He took off his blindfold and ear buds and looked up at her from her lap.

"We've made it to our next stop," she said to him quietly. He nodded and sat up. They stared at each other for a minute though. Verdi remembered. He knew what she had done that no one else had ever done for him. A few hours prior he felt like dying. His sister had put such a pain in his head he thought he would die. Now he was able to think clearly and push aside everything that hurt.

"What?" she said to him with a shrug. Verdi leaned over quickly and kissed her on the cheek.

"Thank you," he said quietly. He opened the door and stepped out of the Humvee for the first time without ear buds or blindfold. She and the others stared for a minute as he walked out onto the brown grass and looked out over the silent city. After a minute they snapped out of it and got out of the vehicle. Anna stayed out with Verdi to watch over him. The others unpacked the car. Anna stayed back a few feet from where Verdi was sitting looking up at the stars.

"You're not stupid," said Verdi after a little while. Anna looked at him with some confusion.

"What did you say?"

"You said, "I'm not as stupid as people like to think I am, Verdi." You're not stupid. I never thought that." Anna walked over and sat next to him.

"I thought you couldn't hear me."

"Bits got through. That bit especially. You were angry." Anna pulled up some of the grass from the ground and looked at it.

"I knew it wasn't a dream," she said considering the grass in her hand.

"What?"

"When you appeared in my nightmare. When you fixed it all and left me in a happy dream about my husband and daughter. I knew."

"I thought you would be angry."

"I wasn't certain. But then I considered the fact that you could have done any number of things to me. You could have made that nightmare infinitely worse. You could have trapped me in that nightmare for as long as you wanted. But you used the memories of my comrades to fix my nightmare. When I sleep now, I don't have that nightmare. If I find myself in that cave, Ismaele and the others come in and get me."

"What you did... no one has ever done."

"I find it kind of surprising that your sister never did that."

"She's the one who put the screaming in my head that you managed to lock behind doors. You're still surprised?"

"I'm an only child, Verdi. As such, I'm jealous of everyone who has siblings. Ever more jealous of twins."

"We never got along."

"You did once though, didn't you?" Verdi looked at her rather taken aback. "It's an only child thing. I can tell."

"How does being an only child help you with that?"

"It's an outside looking in thing. I've seen lots of siblings and the way they interact. She mentioned that you would know." Verdi didn't say anything for a minute.

"There was a time... for a long time we were the best of friends."

174

"What happened?" Anna turned and looked at him now. He had an unreadable expression on his face. It was somewhere between regret and rage.

"We could always hear each other when we were nearby. One day, she shut me out. I couldn't understand it. I tried to talk to her about it, but she wouldn't. It went on like that for three months. One day I cornered her and forced her to let me in. What happened next was... indescribable. I heard her screaming. Just constantly screaming. She had been hurt so badly that all her brain could do was scream. I passed out. When I came to, she had put back up the walls again. As it turned out, it was our father." Anna winced. She didn't like being good at this. She wished she could take it back.

"I take it your father doted on you." Verdi nodded. "For what it's worth, I'm sorry." Verdi took in a deep breath.

"Would you do something for me?"

"What do you have in mind?"

"Play the cello for me?" She looked at him with a confused expression.

"I don't have a cello, Verdi." Verdi looked around for a minute and then went inside. Anna continued to sit on the lawn and stare at the stars. After a few minutes she heard someone clattering at the door and she turned around to see what was going on. Verdi was walking out with a chair, a broom and a ruler.

"What are you doing?" she asked getting up. He sat down the chair near the back of the Humvee and opened the door. He gestured for her to sit down in the chair. She decided to play along and sat in the chair. He then leaned the broom against her left shoulder and handed her the ruler.

"Now, you have a cello. Play the cello."

"This is a broom and a ruler. This is not going to sound like a cello."

"Then sing it."

"There's a reason that I played cello. I can't sing."

"You can sing the tune."

"You already heard me play the cello anyway, why can't we just-"

"That was you pretending. I want to see you remember how you played." Anna sighed. She put her fingers on the broom stick and was slightly surprised how easily her fingers went to the correct positions. The ruler was rectangular and narrow enough that she could almost fool herself into thinking she was holding her bow in her hand. She started to sing quietly as she moved her hands through the positions and bow strokes. She thought of the last time she did this.

She was sitting backstage in jeans and a black t-shirt. She was warming up for a rehearsal. She liked to warm up with Betsy with the first Bach cello suite. They would try to match each other so perfectly in tone and tuning that they would sound like one single cello. That day they were doing particularly well. They moved together in almost perfect synchronicity. Even their head movements were the same. Once they reached the end, the conductor was calling them to rehearsal. Anna dropped the ruler. She had forgotten. This led to somewhere she didn't want to go. This led to a terrible terrible memory.

"What's wrong?" asked Verdi looking at her with an expression of concern and confusion. She dropped the broom and ran into the house. The others tried to talk to her, but she ran past them. She ran into the kitchen and pulled out a bottle of bourbon from under a counter. She cracked it open and took a long swig. Ismaele was walking in cautiously.

"Anna?" he said quietly. She grabbed hold of the bottle and walked away deeper into the building. Verdi walked in and watched her walk away.

"Do you know what's wrong?" asked Ismaele.

"I'm as confused as you!" said Verdi. "I just asked her to remember playing the cello and she was going through a great memory when suddenly she just stopped and ran away. I couldn't see anything past the conductor calling them to rehearsal." They all stared after her. For once since this trip began, no one knew what was going on with their one female companion.

176

# Chapter 13

They made dinner. Ismaele found her drinking on a balcony but couldn't get her to come in and eat. He took a plate up to her after they were all done eating.

"You should eat something," he said quietly to her. "All that liquor in your system with no food is no good. You and I both know that." She took another swig from the bottle and Ismaele saw that it was now half empty. "Look, I'll leave it here, okay?" He sat it down next to the door where she could easily reach it. "Don't let it get too cold now." He walked back inside and downstairs again.

"Did she say anything?" asked Verdi as he came down.

"No, nothing," said Ismaele. "Are you sure you didn't see anything? She didn't say anything?"

"Nothing! I don't know what's gotten her so upset. She was happy. She and Betsy were playing together and they were matching so precisely they nearly sounded like one cello. Then the conductor was calling them to rehearsal and that's when she suddenly just... shut down."

"Maybe something happens after that. Something she doesn't want to remember."

"What could be so bad?"

"You've seen into our minds Verdi. You should know better than to ask that." Verdi realized what he had said and then nodded.

"Where is she?"

"Second floor. Big balcony that comes from the yellow oval room. I don't know if you will have any better luck than me. But you're welcome to try."

"I wouldn't," said Zaccaria from behind them. "There's a reason she doesn't talk about playing anymore."

"Alright genius, tell us. What's gotten her so upset?"

"The last time she played was the day the bombs fell." Both Verdi and Ismaele looked at each other with a look of unbelievable realization. How had they managed to be that stupid?

"Past the conductor, past rehearsal... oh dear God..." Verdi muttered rubbing his forehead.

"She never talks about that day," said Ismaele. "We've all shared stories about it, but never her. And we don't press." Verdi nodded and looked up the stairs. He was being pulled in two directions. One told him to keep his distance and stay downstairs with the others. The other told him to go to her and find out how she was doing. Try to talk to her and extract from her that pain that she had kept hidden from all including her closest companions.

"What do you think-"

"I don't know, Verdi," said Ismaele. "For once I don't know. I'm closer to her than the others. I probably know her better than the others do. Most any other time I'd be able to tell you what to do and what she needs and could probably get it done myself. But she wouldn't even speak to me. Just sat there drinking. I think she tries to keep that memory as far away from her as possible. I think it's just too painful."

"Everyone finds that day painful."

"True. And everyone has dealt with it one way or another. Or never dealt with it. Which is I think what happened with her."

"She lost her husband and her child that day."

"She lost something else that day too. I couldn't tell you what it is to save my life but it's something. Something that she never wanted to lose. That's why she looks sad when she's around Betsy. They both lost it. They're tied together by the same pain. It's kept them close over the years." Verdi finally made a decision and started for the steps. "Shout to us if she gets violent. We'll come running." Verdi nodded quickly and then took off up the steps. It was now or never.

Verdi walked through the wreck of the Yellow Oval Room and out onto the balcony. It was a huge rounded balcony that

178

looked out over a dead city. Anna was sitting there, picking at the remaining food on her plate. Ismaele had made sure to give her several slices of bread to try and counteract the effects of the whiskey. He saw the bottle and saw that it was still half full. She was intoxicated for certain. But not so completely gone that conversation wasn't a possibility. She didn't look up. She was sopping up spaghetti sauce with the sliced wheat bread and eating it slowly. Verdi wanted to say something. Anything. But instead he sat down and waited. It was the smarter move he realized after a few moments. She picked up the bottle and instead of drinking from it, passed it over to him.

"If you expect me to say anything, you need to have a drink first," she said with an edge in her voice. She wanted to say. She needed to say. But she didn't want to say it to anyone who was sober. Verdi opened the bottle and took two long swigs from it before re-corking it and setting it back down. "How are the others?"

"They're worried," said Verdi.

"Right. Because what good is a crying soldier after all?"

"Anna, you know they don't-"

"I do know they don't. I don't like people watching over me so closely. It makes me feel claustrophobic. And like I'm failing. And I know they don't think that either. We've all watched over each other and nursed each other through, something. No one is immune to pain it seems."

"What happened that day? They said you never talk about it."

"There's a reason I don't talk about it. It's too painful to talk about. But I think I've cushioned my brain with enough whiskey that I can get through this conversation without a total mental breakdown." She took another swig from the bottle and ate the last bit of wheat bread. "I was at rehearsal. We were prepping for a really big concert. And we were all so excited. I don't know why we didn't hear the bombs blasting. I really don't know. Other than the fact that we were doing the 1812 overture and were practicing with the cannon blasts. So I guess we didn't even think about it. The lights went out and the emergency lights came on. We were

179

all so entranced by our music. We just didn't stop. We got done with one particularly good and loud run through when one of the ticket guys came running in. He was white faced. We'd never seen him like that before. This was one calm stalwart guy and he was shaking like a leaf. He ran up and told us. He told us that New York had been attacked. Bombs everywhere. No one was certain who was alive and who was dead. No one knew what worked and what didn't. No one was sure of anything. Only thing they were sure of? It wasn't just us. It was multiple cities in America. Then cities in Europe and Asia and Japan and Africa, Russia, Australia... everywhere. No one was immune and in the confusion, no one was sure anymore who struck first, or who had even struck. So we all just went at each other. We sat there. Hearing all of this. The horror of it all. And we realized our lives as we had known them were over. We didn't know what to do. Then Betsy had an idea. She leaned over and told me her idea. We started playing the opening chords of the last movement of the Tchaikovsky's 6th symphony. The other strings started to play with us and the bassoon came in right on cue. We had all played it so many times before we had it memorized. And if one couldn't remember a note or two they would just watch the others. We played through the whole final movement. And we cried. Our conductor just sat down in his chair and cried. He didn't conduct at all. Everyone in the theatre gathered in the hall and held each other. After that, we packed up our instruments. We put them backstage. And we left."

"You left your instruments there?"

"That way of life was dead now. We couldn't be musicians anymore. We couldn't be who we once were. So we left that all behind. We parted ways in front of Carnegie Hall. We went searching through a bombed out and alien like city for those we loved. I found my husband's office building. Or at least, what was left of it. None had escaped. Our daughter's day care was across the street. We had picked it intentionally because if there was ever a problem he could just run across the street and get her. That was when I saw it. The worst thing I've ever seen in my life. He had made it across the street. The day care place had caught fire. I saw teachers holding babies. Burned to a crisp. The screams of the little children almost seemed to echo up from the place. My husband had made it across the street. He was badly hurt though. He made it as far as the sidewalk in front of the day care before collapsing. My daughter had tried to save a baby and a ceiling beam fell on her. She lay on the floor. Her hand just a couple of centimeters from her father's. They died reaching out for one another. I cried. I don't know how long I cried and screamed and shouted at God and the universe for taking them away from me. Sooner or later, I ran out of tears, I ran out of screams and I just couldn't feel anything anymore. I got up and wandered the city. I found a few of my companions again. I found Betsy. All of us had lost someone. No one was immune. No one knew what to do. Betsy had a van. Her two children were dead and I remember how bad I felt when we pulled out her children's car seats and left them on the side of the road so that we could all fit. That was the last time we ever talked about her children. We all piled in and started driving. We got out of New York and into New Jersey. We found a lot of people gathering at various places there. Information and misinformation was flying everywhere. It was hard to get a definite answer to anything. I met up with Izzy there. He was recruiting people to go to the base in Chicago. Well, what was left of Chicago. The base was an abandoned high school. In the end it seemed like the best possible place. Huge kitchen, back up supplies, rooms and rooms to set up bunk beds and house a new army. It was all being run by a guy we all just called Captain. Had no other name for him. He was a good man. A reasonable man. I highly respected him while he was alive. He treated even the new recruits with respect. Many of the people who signed up with me eventually fell out or ran away. Only a few stayed. I didn't even meet Zac and Dallo until the third wave of recruits came through and Izzy and I lost our original two companions."

"You four seem like you've been together forever."

"You wouldn't have thought that if you had seen us when Izzy and I first met the loving couple. We were angry. We were raw. To Zac and Dallo's credit, they did try their hardest to not make it worse. They kept out of our way. They put up with our shit. And one morning we were called directly out of bed to defend the walls. Suddenly, it was like we had fought together our entire lives. We could practically read each other's minds. We won the day and went back to bed." She chuckled now thinking about it. "Kind of a funny reaction in the end. Captain came around to check on us and when he discovered us all sound asleep he left. Waited until we showed up for lunch. I think he was glad that we had finally overcome our awkwardness and become a cohesive unit. After that day, we've almost always been together. Very few times we've split up and then only for a couple of hours. It makes us worried when we're apart."

"That's why they're worried now?"

"Yeah, they don't like me being away from them. At the base I would wander off to abandoned classrooms but they could always find me there and learned my habits quickly. I needed time alone sometimes and they would grant me that. But at the base we were safe and they knew where I would be. Here, no one knows what will happen. It makes them nervous. I bet if you go down there now, they'll be picking rooms close to each other to bed down for the night. Somewhere close enough that they can yell to each other if needed but far away enough that Izzy can't hear the lovers' moans."

"Are they always like this?"

"They've been in bunk beds with the two of us nearby for the last year. Would you want to make hot passionate love to your lover with your two comrades literally five feet away from you?" Verdi nodded in understanding. "I only got them one night to themselves in that whole year. So if they seem excessively randy, they have good cause." Verdi took another sip from the bottle and passed it back to her. She took a sip and corked the bottle again. "So now that you know my great and overwhelming secret, not to mention the secret of which instrument I play, what is your great plan to save the world?" Verdi took the bottle back and took a long swig for courage.

"Music," he said calmly. She blinked.

"I'm sorry, what?"

182

"Music. My great plan is music."

"Music?" She was looking at him with a great amount of doubt and disbelief. "We've nearly gotten killed a few times, friends of ours have been killed, your own sister wants you dead and your big idea... is music?" Verdi felt his resolve slipping but he had to explain. "What just any music? Are you going to play coma-inducing elevator music from loud-speakers for the rest of our lives?!"

"No, I've been composing."

"You've been composing. How in the hell have you managed to do that? Draw your own score paper?"

"No, I've been composing in my head. I remember it all. I've always been able to do this. I just compose things in my head and then write them down later. I just haven't been able to write this one down."

"Great, that's just great. So when we get to New York what's the plan?"

"Carnegie Hall. That little performance space you were imagining. It has a piano, yes?"

"The last time I was there, yes, it had a piano. There are no guarantees that there is one there now or that it's even in tune."

"You said yourself that places of music are often viewed as holy ground. What's more holy than Carnegie Hall?"

"A few places but it does rank high on the list."

"Right, so we get there and use the radio to broadcast this piece that I'm writing. We broadcast it to everyone who will listen. And someone out there is bound to record it and send it out to others. They'll play it and they'll hear it and-"

"And WHAT?! Suddenly we'll be like little kids around the campfire singing Kumbaya? Do you even see the ridiculousness of your plan here Verdi? I mean really? Do you see it?" Anna got up and walked back into the yellow oval room. She was drunk and upset and raw and now the great plan that she had risked and lost nearly everything she had left for was another dud. Verdi followed her in and grabbed her by the arm with a forcefulness

183

she had never seen from him. He was determined though. He had to make her see.

"I have to make everyone see the hurt that everyone is in. I have to make them see the rage and pain and the grief! And I have to make them see that it can be fixed. That this can all be fixed." Anna started to laugh cynically.

"You think you can influence men's minds with music? Really?" He pulled her through the room and into the President's bedroom. There was still a bed and a few sticks of furniture. He sat her down on the bed and said to her very clearly,

"You of all people should know that's true." He put his iPod in the speaker he still carried around and started playing the last movement of Tchaikovsky's sixth symphony. Immediately her face went ashen and she jumped for the speaker. But he held her back with his spindly arms.

"No! Turn that off!"

"Right, now tell me that music doesn't affect men's minds! Tell me now that it won't grind salt into wounds! That it won't soothe those wounds as well!"

"TURN IT OFF VERDI DAMN YOU!! TURN IT OFF!" He reached over and paused the song. She stopped struggling with him and leaned into his embrace. "I can't stand to hear that..." she whispered in his shoulder. "I can't stand to hear that piece anymore. If I hear it... all I see is that day." She pulled away from him, sat back down on the bed and sighed slowly. He reached over and picked another piece.

"Tell me what this feels like." It was Erik Satie's Gymnopedie no. 1. She took a deep breath and could almost feel her own fingers hitting the keys. She had learned the piece so long ago.

"Calming, sweet. Sad. I played the piano before I played cello. I always loved to play this piece. Especially when I was feeling blue." The piece played all the way to the end and faded out.

"And this?" He pushed the button for another song. It took her a minute to remember and then she recognized Vivaldi's Four Seasons. It was the first movement of the Winter section.

"Hurried. Racing. Panicked. Have to get somewhere in a hurry for some reason that no one ever found out." She smiled as the music changed.

"And then?"

"He got there. Don't know what it was but the mission was a success." He reached over and searched for another piece as the last one was ending. He pushed the button and she recognized the low first notes of The Firebird Suite. She snickered quietly. "Firebird Suite. The creature reborn in flames. Trying to make a point here are we?" She took a sip from the whiskey bottle and handed the bottle to Verdi. He took a sip as well and recorked the bottle.

"Yes, I am." She looked at him like she had just seen him.

"Liquor makes you braver does it?"

"It does, as a matter of fact. Music affects people. It makes them feel and makes them realize what they are feeling. I think this could work. I think people will hear what I'm going to play and some of them... hopefully enough of them will turn and realize what they're doing and change their minds."

"So, what are you writing? Some great piano sonata? What the subject?"

"It's everything. All the stories that you've told me, all the memories I've gleaned, all the pain and joy and sadness and rage and hope that I've absorbed from all of you. Everyone I've traveled with I've added to this piece."

"This should be one hell of a piece then."

"I hope." Anna took another sip.

"God I'm drunk. I haven't been this drunk in a very long while. And don't start; you don't want to know why I was this drunk the last time."

"Fair enough."

"You already know don't you?"

"You thought about it as you said it. So yes, I know."

"It's got to be hell being you."

"You have no idea." Verdi took a very long drink from the bottle and set it down on the floor. Anna looked at him for a moment considering a question. "Just go ahead and ask it so I can answer you."

"Your sister never did what I did for you?"

"No. Not once. She likes to put screaming demons in my head and set off mental traps that I've left for myself so that I end up in just as much pain as her. She's never tried to fix the mental traps. And yes I did try to help her. I tried several times. But she would use that connection to set off all the demons in my head. After a while, I stopped trying. And I feel bad about that every day of my life."

"You miss her, don't you?"

"I miss her... I miss her in ways I can't describe. It's like missing a limb. She used to be the only one I could talk to when the voices I heard got to be too much. She used to help me shut the world out."

"She did help you."

"She would help me shut out the world, not my inner demons. Shutting out the world is a little easier. It's only happened a couple other times with a couple others."

"How did they do that?"

"Well, I was having sex with them." Anna looked at him in mild shock. "Yes, I have had sex. And yes, I am extremely selective about my lovers for obvious reasons. That's also why in my whole 32 years I've only had two lovers."

"How did it end with those two?"

"Found out one was cheating. The other died when the bombs fell."

"I'm sorry." Verdi studied his shoes very hard. Then glanced at the bottle. Then he felt gentle lips on his cheek as Anna gave him a quick kiss. "I really am, very sorry." Their fingers interlaced together. "Tell me about her." He took in a long shuddering breath and his long-held pain finally came tumbling out.

"She was beautiful. Long black hair, green eyes. She had a way about her that was unlike anyone I had ever known before. She took care of me. She understood me better than most ever did. And she was the only one who could silence the demons my

186

sister would let loose in me... until you." He reached out and touched her cheek gently. They kissed softly and tentatively.

They laid down together on the bed facing each other. Their limbs instinctively wrapped around each other and they held each other close. But then they hesitated. And they both felt it.

"You're drunk," whispered Verdi.

"So are you," she muttered back. "I don't want to sleep alone tonight." He gently kissed her on the forehead.

"Then don't." He reached up and pulled the covers down on the bed. The both of them crawled under the covers together and curled up together. She rested her head on Verdi's chest and slowly went to sleep listening to his heartbeat. Verdi fell asleep soon after.

~

Anna found herself in the theater. It was dim. She was sitting in the front row. She looked up and saw Verdi sitting at the piano. He was perfectly still. She sat forward and stared at him. Verdi was shaking. The bench he was sitting on was practically vibrating.

"What's wrong Verdi?" she asked quietly. She knew this hall. Even her soft words rang through the hall. He looked at her in shock.

"What are you doing here?" he said looking at her.

"I suspect I slipped in accidentally," she said calmly. "Or you slipped into my dream. Either way, we're both here now. Might as well do some good. What are you doing?"

"I'm trying to save the world."

"Wow, that's difficult. How do you intend to do that?"

"By playing the piano."

"Ah, so you're here to give a concert."

"No, to-

"To **give** a concert, Verdi." She saw his shoulders start to ease. "That's all you have to do. Saving the world is far too difficult a task." She got up from her seat and walked towards the stage. "Do you need a page turner?" He looked up and saw the music he had been writing in his head. All of it finally written down

187

and waiting for him on paper. He turned the page and saw solid music.

"I do." She vaulted herself up onto the stage and stood next to him. He put his fingers to the keys. His hands still shook. They both looked up as the doors to the recital hall rattled. Her eyes narrowed and chains and padlocks appeared on the handles. She put a gentle hand on his shoulder.

"Just start playing love," she said quietly. "It's going to be alright." He put his fingers to the keys and began to play. She felt the rage and anger in the music. It was the first section of the piece. The doors rattled further. "Don't worry about them," she whispered close to his ear. "No matter what happens, keep playing." He looked up for a second as he saw them break the chains and break in. He looked back to the music and kept playing. Anna drew a knife and jumped off the stage. The demons were somewhere halfway between men and beasts. They were armed with swords and knives. Anna landed with her companions behind her. Ismael carried a Viking style axe. Abadallo carried a scimitar and Zaccaria a broadsword out of Scotland. They grinned a murderous grin at the surprised demons.

"Oh, you thought I would come alone did you?" said Anna. A fight of immense proportion began as the music continued to play. They fought and the music filled the air. It was a glorious battle. When the last demon fell, Verdi was still playing. Anna turned back to the stage. Now she found she was alone. Verdi was now dressed in a tuxedo and her in the red dress again. She looked around and saw an audience. She looked back at the shut doors. Ismael, Abadallo and Zaccaria were sitting in the front row of the audience in tuxedos now. She walked up the steps at the side of the stage in her bare feet and reached the piano in time to make the first page turn. He stopped playing. She looked at him and he stared back at her.

"Can't play the whole thing and ruin it for you, can I?" He took her hand and pulled her down to the piano bench. He kissed her passionately and she responded in kind. That was when they both woke up kissing on the bed. This time, they didn't hesitate.

They pulled off each other's clothes and were soon naked. That was when she learned exactly why Verdi hardly ever had any lovers. All the skin contact caused him to feel everything she was feeling and everything that he was feeling flowed into her.

"Oh good... God!" she shouted realizing what was going on.

"Sorry," he muttered trying to back off. But she pulled him closer to her.

"No don't," she said quickly running her fingers through his hair. "It just surprised me, I'm not upset." She pulled him down to kiss her again. Soon he was deep inside her and they had lost all ability to form words in the English language. Both of their brains were on overload. Waves of pleasure and passion flowed back and forth between the two of them. Anna understood as they were starting to lose control. She couldn't sense anything around them anymore. She didn't even feel like they were on the same planet. As they both cried out, the only thing they could feel was their limbs wrapped around each other. They were safe and loved and protected as they fell into the dark.

Meanwhile…

Quinn and her men had arrived in New York. The city that once bustled and shone at night was now eerily quiet. Everything was quiet. Even Verdi was quiet. She tried reaching out to him through their old connection but she couldn't. He was quiet and closed off. She knew there was only one way that he could shut out the world.

"Lucky bastard," she muttered to herself. "At least one of us is getting some." She got out of the Humvee and looked out over the silent dark city. "Come morning, he will at least have one last happy memory to hold onto." Her smile was sinister. But one treacherous tear rolled down her cheek.

# Chapter 14

The next morning Ismaele knocked on the door of the bedroom. Anna woke up and looked about. Verdi was still asleep. She wrapped herself in the sheet. Verdi pulled the comforter around him a little tighter as she slipped away. She walked to the door and opened it. Ismaele raised an eyebrow.

"Please," she said in a voice thick was sarcasm. "After all we've been through, you're going to judge me on this?"

"We need to get moving. Get him up."

"Ten minutes." She shut the door back and turned back to the bed. Wrapped in the comforter, he looked so fragile and innocent. She sat down on the bed and shook him gently.

"Verdi, it's time to get up." He groaned audibly and turned over. He looked at her through half-lidded eyes.

"How much longer until we get to New York?"

"It's about a four hour drive. We'll need a little time to get to the recital hall and set up the broadcast equipment."

"So, you're going along with my plan?"

"I've gone along with 33 other save the world plans. I knew most of them wouldn't work. But I still went along with them, just as willingly."

"Do you think this one will work?" Anna turned his hand so that it was palm up in front of her.

"I don't know. I don't know that it will fail though." He smiled and sat up.

"From you, that almost sounds like a vote of confidence." He stroked her cheek, kissed her lips and they pressed their foreheads together. As they pulled away, his expression looked sad. Anna knew something wasn't right. But he wasn't going to tell her. They got dressed and went down to meet the others in the kitchen. They were piecing together breakfast from the supplies in the truck. Mostly canned fruit and bagels. They stopped eating when Anna and Verdi walked in. Anna stared back at them.

"Have something to say boys?"

"You okay?" asked Abadallo.

"Fine. Whiskey and good sex can cure just about anything." She opened a can of pears and stabbed at them with a fork. Verdi picked out a cinnamon bagel and began to nibble on it.

"Right, so Verdi, what's your big plan?" said Zaccaria.

"I need to get to Carnegie Hall in New York," said Verdi. "Once we get there, Anna knows the recital hall I want to go to. I want to play a piece that I've been composing and broadcast it to anyone who is listening." All except Anna stared at him.

"And?" said Ismaele.

"And that's it," said Verdi. "I think that music will change everyone's minds."

"Music?" said Abadallo.

"Yes." The three men looked at Anna who was still staring into her can of pears. Abadallo cleared his throat and she looked up at them.

"He told me last night," she said taking a bite off the pear half on her fork.

"And?"

"And I think it's just crazy enough that it might work. Would like to remind you all it's no crazier than the other missions we've gotten involved in."

"But no mission has cost us more," said Ismaele with a growl. Anna knew that tone.

"I know that. And I was angry when he told me too. I can't say that it will work, but I can't say that it won't either. And I believe that we owe it to everyone we've lost to at least see if this will work. If it doesn't work… we'll kill him." Verdi dropped his bagel. She turned and looked at him with a wicked grin. The others chuckled at his reaction. She handed him a fresh bagel and kissed him on the cheek. "Had to do it. You should have seen the look on your face!"

"All right, all right," he said with a sheepish smirk. After breakfast they packed up their things, turned off the generators to the house and loaded up in the Humvee.

"Where's your iPod?" she asked as they got in.

"In the bag," Verdi replied. "Don't need it right now."

"I figured you'd want it now more than ever."

"No, I need to listen." Anna nodded and sat down in the driver's seat. She turned the key and started the Humvee for the last leg of their trip.

~

The drive was quiet. They didn't talk. Verdi could feel them all thinking though as they watched the desolate landscape go by. All of them were sad and angry. Anna kept looking for landmarks and not finding them. The others did the same. It was two hours before anyone said anything.

"Would you look at a map and make sure we're still on the right path?" said Anna to Abadallo who was sitting next to her in the passenger seat. He pulled out the map from his pack and checked where they were on their path.

"Yeah, you're right," he said after a few minutes.

"This place just looks… wrong." She stared out the windows at a blank landscape. All the buildings were blown away. Soon they could see the remaining charred buildings of New York ahead of them. Anna slowed to a stop.

"Home sweet home," she whispered. "Let's check and see how bad off we are." Abadallo pulled out the Geiger counter in the glove box. It crackled in a worrying way but he said,

"Considering what this city has been through, we're safe for a couple of hours." She turned back and looked at Verdi.

"You ready for this?" He gave her a quick nod. His eyes were full of fear and determination. She turned back and looked at the blown out buildings and wreckage that was once her city.

"Right, let's do this thing." She put her foot back on the gas pedal and they rolled into the city.

It didn't take long before she started recognizing the roads and paths she used to take. Coming off the New Jersey Turnpike she almost felt like she was on autopilot. As they approached the

Lincoln Tunnel, Verdi put a hand to her shoulder. She slowed to a stop.

"What is it?" He peered into the dark of the tunnel.

"I don't know," he said quietly. "This place always scared me. Looks even worse with all the safety lights gone." She flipped on the high beams. They could see the wreckage in the tunnel. Cars abandoned or stripped or husks of cars that had burned out long ago. "Do you think we can make it all the way through?" The others now craned their necks and stared into the dark.

"This is the quickest way to Carnegie Hall," she said calmly. "The Lincoln Bridge got taken out with the bombs and I'm not sure that we can get to any of the other bridges or if they're still there. This is our best shot."

"If we get too stuck, we can get out and shift the cars a bit," said Ismaele. "I vote for the tunnel."

"Sorry, Verdi," said Zaccaria. "I'm for the tunnel too." Abadallo nodded as well.

"Alright," said Verdi with a sigh. "Tunnel it is. Just be careful." Anna slowly rolled forward. It was very slow going for the most part. She sped through what few open sections there were and crawled through close turns. They were about ten minutes into their slow crawl when the tunnel was blocked. Ismaele, Zaccaria and Abadallo got out. Two cars met bumper to bumper in the middle. Zaccaria put one into neutral and they were able to push it to the side. Anna slowly crawled forward through the space.

"Just keep it slow, we'll stay out in case there's any more trouble," said Ismaele. She nodded and made sure they kept in her line of sight as they crawled along. Five minutes later they had to roll a couple more cars out of the way. She looked back at Verdi.

"You okay?" she asked.

"I'm alright," he said with a quick nod.

"Still got that weird feeling about this place?"

"This whole place feels weird. It's too... quiet. I used to hate coming into the city because it was so loud. So many people made it nearly impossible to walk down the street. I used to dream of this place being quiet. Now that I have that wish, I would give anything to take it back." She wasn't sure what to say to him. So she reached back and gave his hand a brief squeeze.

"Maybe one day it won't be quiet anymore." She continued to navigate the vehicle through the wreckage. They were starting to see the end of the tunnel when Verdi's hand came down on her shoulder hard. She looked back and saw the strain and pain on his face.

"Hurry," he whispered. She leaned out the window.

"Everyone, back in the truck we have to go NOW!!" They didn't question. They got into the truck and she put the pedal to the floor. They busted through the last two cars and made it out of the tunnel to see daylight. She careened through the curve onto Dyer Ave.

"What the hell Anna?" shouted Ismaele falling over himself in the back.

"It's Quinn!! She's somewhere nearby!!" Anna shouted back. The others looked at Verdi and saw the pain on his face. Zaccaria jumped into the back with Ismaele and they opened the window. They both loaded their rifles and scanned the horizon as it sped away from them. Anna nearly flipped the whole vehicle at the turn onto 42nd. Verdi's grip on her shoulder never loosened.

"Stay with me Verdi," she muttered to him. She covered his hand with hers and said again, "Stay with me. We're almost there. I swear we are almost there. Do you boys see anything?"

"Nothing so far," said Ismaele. Neither of them looked away. She slammed on the brakes and turned onto 8th Ave.

"This is going to be the longest stretch so keep watch!" Abadallo watched the side streets as they flew past. But he didn't see anyone. There was no one in the whole city but them. But Verdi continued to look like he was in the worst pain of his life. Anna kept looking down side streets. She stared at the horizon. But there was no one. She nearly missed and then made the turn onto 57th and the subsequent turn onto 7th avenue. She braked hard in front of the far left door which she knew led to the recital hall he wanted.

"We're here!! Quick, everyone out!! Grab the radio!!" She got out of the Humvee and opened the door next to Verdi. She took his face in her hands and turned his face to her. His eyes found their focus and he seemed to look right through her. She said in a calm and firm voice, "We're here. Let's get going." He nodded slowly. He pulled together what was left of his mental and physical strength and slowly stepped out of the car. Anna put his arm around her shoulders and she half carried him into the building. Ismaele ran in front, gun pointed, radio at his side and the long-saved bottle of scotch in his cargo pants pocket.
 Abadallo kept close to Verdi and Anna while Zaccaria covered them from behind as they walked through the building. The place was almost exactly the same as she remembered it. There was a light film of dust. The halls were dark and their flashlights cut through like blades. She kicked open the door to the recital hall.
 They were all shocked to the see the grand piano still sitting there like not a day had passed. All the chairs, however, had been ripped and torn out. People who were desperate for something to burn and something to make them comfortable had taken them long ago. Anna walked him from the door and up the steps to the stage. She sat him down on the piano stool and took his face in his hands again.

"Remember Verdi, remember why we're here." His eyes were looking up at her like she was someone he was supposed to remember. "Verdi? C'mon you okay?" Ismaele put down the radio and the generator and fired it up. He tuned to an open channel that he knew everyone transmitted freely on while Anna tried to reach Verdi. "Verdi? Talk to me kid, please!" Verdi grabbed hold of her hand and squeezed very hard.

"She's... here..." he whispered.

"Testing, one two three," said Ismaele into the radio receiver. "If anyone is out there, keep on this channel and tell everyone you know to turn to it. We've got some Saturday afternoon music for you today." The doors busted open and Quinn was standing there. Men were behind her. Big, burly, well-armed men. Ismaele put the radio on the piano and put a rubber band around the receiver to hold the button in position. He looked at Anna who nodded to him.  She pulled away from Verdi even though she felt his fingers trying to grab hold of her.  She stepped around the piano stool and stared straight at Quinn.

"You said we could continue this conversation here," said Quinn with an evil smirk.  "This seems to be as good of a time as any."

"Let him try at least," said Anna with a bit more begging in her voice than she had intended.

"Hmm, how about... no?"  The men behind her ran forward with a roar.  Abadallo, Zaccaria, Ismaele and Anna all opened fire on them.  The men kept coming.  Only two fell.  They were trampled to jelly underneath their companions' feet.  Those who were still running swung knives and axes.  Ismaele dropped to the floor and took the biggest man down with a bullet to the head.  He took the Viking-esque battle axe from his dead hands and began to swing it wildly at their opponents.  Zaccaria and Abadallo stood back to back.  Fresh out of bullets, they had resorted to knives and punches.

Anna dived into the fray and took out one brute who was about to stab Ismaele from behind.  She slipped through the men heading for her one target: the red head running at her from the back.  The two met in the middle of the floor.  They were each armed with a large knife.  They danced around each other and made passes and swipes at each other.  Anna dived one of Quinn's thrusts and rolled back up to a standing position.  She swung her arm around and her knife was at Quinn's throat at the same moment that she felt the cold steel of Quinn's blade at hers.  In that second, above it all, they all heard one voice scream out,

"NOOOOOOOOOO!!!"  Then the angry sound of a piano chord being slammed too hard on the keys.  The piano wheezed and whined in protest.  But this was answered only by a second and then third dissonant and angry chord.  Everyone was frozen in place.  The chords continued.  Jumbled, crazed and insane chords that were filled with too many notes and too many dissonances.  Intervals that made Anna's ears ache and made her face screw up in a wince even though the rest of her did not move.

Soon there were notes.  Notes in between the chords.  Hurried and frightened notes that ran across the strings like mice escaping a hawk.  The piano groaned under the strain.  The angry chords still punctuated the running and fleeing of the quicker lighter notes.  Like some giant stomping on an ant hill.

The chords began to lessen.  More consonance than dissonance now.  But still in a minor key.  The tempo slowed.  Anna could feel her heart slow with it.  She saw Quinn's shoulder start to relax.  She should have taken it as an opportunity to strike.  But she didn't.

The skittering notes slowed to a sad and somber melody.  It drifted and flowed across the piano as if blown by the wind.  More notes joined.  The melody was thickened with painful diminished chords that came up from the bottom.  It was a dirge.  A massive funeral dirge for everyone that had been lost.  Anna's and Quinn's arms slowly dropped to their sides in an almost synchronized movement.  But neither could stop staring at the other.  The music continued.

The dirge turned.  The chords that had drug everything down now began to lift.  Slowly they became simple minor chords under a tune that sounded more hopeful than funereal.  The melody was left alone.  A tiny white dove drifting through the sky in search of a home.  The countermelody, another tiny dove flew with it.  They dived and peaked and rose on the wind.  The chords returned to buoy them upwards and help them to reach the sky.  The music increased in tempo again.  The birds flew around each other in barrel rolls and joyous dives.

Anna finally looked away from Quinn and saw Verdi.  He was at the piano.  His fingers practically danced across the keys.  His eyes were tight shut remembering every single note that he had written for this specific moment.  For these people to hear so that maybe, maybe they would hear and turn and come together.  Maybe this would finally bring the people back together again.  He didn't know if this would work.  He never knew.  But this was what he could do.  And he knew how to do it well.

Across the country, radios were crackling and straining under the great sound of the piano in New York. People everywhere were frozen. They couldn't stop listening. They didn't want to stop listening. There was something about this piece. Something that they couldn't quite put their finger on. A few who were smart enough like Snake were recording it. They wanted to hear it again and again. They wanted to figure out what it was with this piece. Why it was important. How it was important. They weren't sure. All they knew was that it was, in that moment, the most important thing in the world. It made them all feel better.

Quinn now turned and watched her brother, her twin brother, playing the piano with every bit of strength that he had left in his body. The melody swelled and rose and seemed to bust her heart open and she fell to her knees at the sheer beauty of it. He looked up at her and smiled. The old connection that they had since childhood fired again and he reached out to her across the room. The screaming pain she had held so long to herself he finally healed. She thought she could almost hear his voice in her head saying,

"I told you I could help." Tears streamed down her cheeks and she wished she had never cut him out of her life.

He looked to Anna and the others who had carried him so far and risked it all and lost so much and smiled. He eased their hurts and calmed their tempers. He nodded to them in thanks for bringing him here and helping him to achieve this. He turned back to the keys and his hands danced through the last few lines. The chords slipped away first. Followed by the countermelody. Finally only the lonely sweet melody of hope drifted across the keys and ended on one final note that everyone everywhere had to strain to hear. He laid his hands down in his lap and shut his eyes. No one in the hall dared breathe. Everyone, Anna, her friends, Quinn, her men, all of them stood stock still, dumbfounded. Verdi didn't move. He was still sitting on the piano stool.

"You're supposed to take a bow, now," Anna said so quietly that it was hardly above a whisper. But in that hall everyone heard her words. They all turned and stared straight at

Verdi. But Verdi still didn't move. Anna felt her heart sink through her chest. She slowly walked towards the stage. The others all continued to stare at him. She walked up the side steps of the stage and slowly walked over to the piano. She stood next to the piano and said, "I said, you're supposed to take a bow now. You have to get up and receive the thanks of your audience." Verdi didn't move. His eyes remained shut. Anna felt tears welling up in her eyes as she reached out to touch him. "Please..." She touched his cheek. He didn't react. Her hand drifted to his neck and she felt no pulse. "Please..." She sunk to her knees and touched his knee. She heard someone nearby crying and she turned and saw Quinn standing at the edge of the stage. She walked over to her twin and wrapped her arms around his shoulders. She stroked his hair and kissed him gently on the temple.

"Good night Andrew," she whispered.

"Why?" said Anna through the tears that were choking her words.

"It was all he had left," said Quinn still cradling her twin brother. "All that he had left to give. He risked everything to try and reach everyone. He was keeping inside himself the pain and sorrow and hope of everyone he had ever met. He put it all into a piece and made certain that anyone who was listening to him play it, would stop wherever they were and listen. He used his abilities to heal everyone he could reach. And now..." She couldn't finish her sentence and instead continued to cry. Anna stood. She looked from Verdi's body to Quinn to the men standing near the edge of the stage. All of them in tears whether they understood why or not. Anna turned off the radio. She passed it to Ismaele who put it on the floor. She helped Quinn lift her brother off the piano stool and lay him on the floor. Quinn kneeled next to his body.

"What should we do?" asked Quinn looking at Anna like a lost child.

"We give him the burial he deserves," Anna replied. She turned around and grabbed the battle axe out of Ismaele's hands. With a giant roar that came out of some great and savage place within her being, she swung the axe at the piano and the cover splintered in half. Quinn grabbed another axe from one of her men and with an equal scream of rage and sorrow swung. The men stepped back. Not out of fear, but out of reverence. They stood quietly and solemnly with axes, blades and guns at their sides. It was not their place to help. It was their place to keep silent guard. Keys flew, wood splintered, the strings twisted and snapped under the pressure of the two women's shared anger and pain. Finally, when the piano and the accompanying bench were in splinters, they threw down their axes. They lifted Verdi onto the wreckage and set him in a place of honor where he was cradled by the body of the piano itself. Ismaele handed Anna the bottle of scotch. She took a drink and Quinn took a drink before they poured the remaining contents onto the makeshift funeral pyre that they had created. They stepped back and took one last long look. Anna pulled out her lighter and her last package of cigarettes. She took one and then offered the pack to Quinn. Quinn took one and held it to her lips. Anna lit her cigarette, lit Quinn's cigarette and then lit the trail of liquor on the floor. The blue flames ran across the stage like the notes across the page.

 The piano caught fire quickly and consumed Verdi with it. The two women jumped down from the stage and led the men out of the building. By the time they reached the doors of the hall, the fire had reached the walls. By the time they reached the outside doors, the fire had consumed the hall. And by the time that they had loaded into their cars and started to make their way together to the Terzu province, the whole building was on fire and falling to the ground. Anna was the only one who looked back.

Made in the USA
Las Vegas, NV
11 February 2022